HIT AND RUN

A new novel from this master story-teller

Luke Grant enjoys his comfortable life with his dog, his outdoor pursuits and his numerous female companions. But when the widowed wife of his grandson is badly injured in a hit-and-run accident, it is down to Luke (or G.G. - great-grand-dad - as he's known) to take on looking after his great-granddaughters and to try and find out who - and why - injured his granddaughter.

Gerald Hammond titles available from Severn House Large Print

Loving Memory
Waking Partners
Keeper Turned Poacher
On the Warpath
Colds in the Heads
The Outpost

HIT AND RUN

Gerald Hammond

Severn House Large Print
London & New York

This first large print edition published 2009
in Great Britain and the USA by
SEVERN HOUSE PUBLISHERS LTD of
9-15 High Street, Sutton, Surrey, SM1 1DF.
First world regular print edition published 2008 by
Severn House Publishers Ltd., London and New York.

British Library Cataloguing in Publication Data

Hammond, Gerald, 1926-
  Hit and run.
  1. Great-grandfathers--Family relationships--Fiction.
  2. Hit-and-run drivers--Fiction. 3. Detective and mystery
  stories. 4. Large type books.
  I. Title
  823.9'14-dc22

ISBN-13: 978-0-7278-7810-6

Printed and bound in Great Britain by
MPG Books Ltd, Bodmin, Cornwall.

One

Looking back, Luke Grant thought that he should perhaps have been nicknamed Lucky like the fugitive Lord Lucan, or Lucky Jim in the Kingsley Amis novel. He seemed to have led a charmed life. He had made mistakes. He had had accidents. Who hadn't? But mistakes and accidents of a kind that had spelled disaster for others had proved less damaging or sometimes had even turned out to be advantageous for him.

His mother had chosen the name because she was too busy with her career as a sculptor to fritter away precious time and mental energy on name-choosing. After naming her first two sons Mathew and Mark, Luke seemed a logical follow-on. Luke's younger sister was named Joanna. At that point, due to the death of his father under the wheels of a Carter Paterson lorry, procreation in that generation of the Grant family ceased, or God knows where it might have led.

Luke was born near Newton Lauder, in the Scottish Borders, around the time of the General Strike. His performance at school was no better than average in the academic subjects. He might have shone at pictorial art. He knew precisely where each line should be placed and he knew the value of every tone and tint. He understood the play of light and shade and the precise positioning of subjects alive or dead to betoken movement. More than that, he knew how mood should be portrayed. Unfortunately, his hand would not do his bidding and what was so clear in his mind only appeared on the paper or canvas as if seen through a glass, darkly. As a draughtsman he was a failure. He might have painted abstracts but he despised much of modern art; moreover, he was sadly aware that artists such as Pablo Picasso and Salvador Dali were in fact superb draughtsmen. His only other talent was as a gymnast. He might have risen high in that world but at that time there was hardly a living to be made in it. He would have looked for sponsorship to underwrite a training programme with the Olympics in mind, but World War Two had intervened.

When he became old enough to enlist Luke, in a fever of patriotism, volunteered for the army. On his first leave from Lanark, where he had been posted for basic training, the girl from a nearby farmhouse, Hannah Mc-Pherson, succumbed at last to his good looks and blandishments in the summer-house behind his parents' house.

He would have made a good officer. He was singled out for officer training. Before his posting to OCTU at Heysham he was sent on leave. It now emerged that Hannah was expecting his child. A hasty marriage was arranged, performed and, when Hannah succumbed again, consummated.

During his time at OCTU an accident brought an end to his military career. An instructor engaged in teaching the officer cadets how to knock out an enemy tank was carrying a two-pound PIAT mortar bomb over slippery rocks, wearing studded army boots. The result was predictable. He dropped a bomb at Luke's feet and his own. The instructor was killed. Luke lost part of his right foot and a splinter took out his right eye.

After consideration, the army decided that he was no longer of use to it. His own training had not been so far advanced that he could train others and his damaged foot prevented his employment as a PT instructor. He was invalided out, back to Civvy Street, with a disability pension and a scarred face. It was a serious accident, but in view of the slaughter that happened to his regiment on D Day, it may have saved his life.

He had given some consideration to becoming an art critic. As an adjunct to that activity he renewed an earlier interest in photography. The system of government grants for returning servicemen was already in place and by making full use of the facility he took an advanced course. The chemistry and technology came easily to him but it was his intuitive understanding of composition and his ability to catch and express a mood that marked him out from his fellows. He could recognize and anticipate the precise instant when the picture would be perfect and grab it before it escaped. Of a sudden, he had found a career that was open to a one-eyed man with a limp.

Of his siblings, Mark had been lost to a German sniper and Mathew was aboard a destroyer hit squarely by a kamikaze pilot.

Joanna was a member of the Land Army and was about to marry a farmer in Wales. His mother was happy to welcome her surviving son along with his very new family back into the family home and to allow him to convert a former scullery into a darkroom. Some excellent equipment was to be had, second-hand.

His career blossomed from the start. The war was ending but the rush of returning servicemen had not begun, so he had the field largely to himself, sharing it only with the old and the very young. New periodicals were springing up whenever the paper was to be had, bringing with them new technology and a growing market for good photography. A win in a major and much-publicised competition brought him to the attention of advertising agencies and picture editors. They soon found out that it took only a few words of ill-expressed guidance for him to produce exactly the picture that they thought they had wanted all along. His wife, aided by his mother when the latter was between sculpting commissions, proved perfectly capable of looking after the baby – and each other – during his absences. During quiet periods, country walks often provided opportunities for wildlife photography and he was sometimes referred to by newspapers, magazines or even the new-fangled television wanting shots of specific wildlife from his growing collection. One photograph that was never published he obtained by chance while walking on upper Deeside hoping for a shot of an osprey. He passed a young lady whom he recognized as a minor princess, walking, for once, alone. Glancing round he saw that she had the back of her skirt tucked into her knickers. He warned her, of course, but not until he had taken a colour shot. The media even then had lost their reverence for royalty and would have paid handsomely for it; Luke, on the other hand, still respected them for attempting an impossibly difficult job. He suppressed the shot in exchange for a promise of privileged access to all royal occasions at Balmoral.

The years rolled by. His mother died and he inherited the family home. Despite his frequent absences when he and his cameras were required in far-flung parts of the globe, he contrived to father a brother for Simone.

Luke nursed Hannah through a terminal

cancer and wept when she died. But life must go on. He had contrived, with the help of a neighbour, to raise his two children. His daughter, Simone, established the family tradition by marrying young. Luke found himself a grandfather at forty-three.

Simone's only son, Henry, returned from his parents' farm in Sutherland to take up a legal apprenticeship in Newton Lauder. As impetuous as his grandfather, he embarked on an affair with the daughter of a local bank manager. When they married, Luke and the bride's father combined to help them towards the purchase of a house not far from Luke's house, *Ceilidh*. It might have made economic sense if Luke had offered them a share of his home, which was quite large enough to house a growing family as well as a widower, but Luke had reservations about that marriage. He considered the bride, Emily, to be a tartar who had every intention of soon wearing the trousers. Additionally, sharing his home might have made it difficult for Luke to entertain his occasional visitors.

Thus it came about that Luke was a great-grandfather at the age of sixty-four. He was still very fit. He thought that he might yet see the first of his great-great-grand-children.

Emily did turn out to be a bossy-boots but Luke needed to see very little of her and Henry was spared much of her domination. Henry, having changed careers by now, was often abroad as a respected journalist and later died when an aircraft hit an alp, just after his second daughter was born. He left his widow provided for at a level that many would have considered satisfactory but which she found to be a subject of complaint.

Their houses were a mile and a half apart; Luke's in the country and Emily's in a small offshoot from Newton Lauder. This enabled him to stay in touch with the girls for years without making more than minimal contact with their mother, which suited all parties.

The phone call caught Luke hard at work. He had long since turned almost all of his photography over to digital systems although the old-fashioned film camera was still essential for very close-up work when precise focusing was necessary and for sporting shots for which even the least shutter delay was unacceptable. His small darkroom could not accommodate both activities and so his mother's former sculpture studio had been converted for the purpose. To take a photograph may occupy as little as a thousandth of a second but that instant must be followed by seemingly endless tasks. He had to feed the contents of his camera's memory into his computer, identify each shot, process each image for zoom, cropping, colour value, red-eye and ever more sophisticated stages of titivation. He had to email off images to various clients, make prints for others, index them and burn his finished images onto recordable CDs. At a later stage came the preparation of accounts, VAT returns and all the red tape that money gathers around it.

At the sound of the musical summons he straightened his back stiffly and stretched out for his mobile phone. One thing about digital, a computer usually could be left to itself when conventional prints would have spoiled.

The voice sounded brisk and efficient but momentarily subdued. 'Mr Grant? Mr Luke Grant? Am I right in thinking that Violet and Jane Highsmith are your granddaughters?'

'Almost but not quite,' he said. 'They're my great-granddaughters. What is this? Who are you?'

'I'm Sister Macintyre. I'm speaking from A and E at the hospital.'

He caught his breath. 'Nothing's happened to one of the girls?'

The voice hesitated. 'I'm sorry,' it said. 'I can't discuss it on the phone. But it isn't the girls. Can you come in, please?'

This sounded serious. He glanced around the state of the work. 'I'll be there in about twenty minutes.'

He spent a necessary few minutes tidying and storing his work so far and another five tidying himself. While he was alone at home, he was inclined to let the niceties of personal appearance slide. He changed his shoes and passed a hand over his chin. He needed a shave but since his hair had lost its pigment he could get away with shaving on alternate days. He whistled up his Labrador. He could not know for how long he would be away. His Land Rover was at the door. It was long past its prime but typical for the neighbourhood. It started at the first turn of the switch. He pulled out into what was in fact a farm road but better surfaced than

14

many of its kind. Emerging from the trees onto the B-road that served the area, he set the Land Rover to climb, grumbling, up a steep hill through open country to the hospital.

Sister Macintyre was waiting for him at the desk in A and E. She had sounded brusque on the phone but in person she looked kindly. Luke guessed her age at thirty-five. 'Mr Grant?' she said. She paused. 'No, you can't be. You don't look old enough to be anybody's great-grandparent, let alone a girl of sixteen.'

'You should see the picture in the attic. I'm eighty-one,' Luke said, not without a touch of pride.

'Well, you don't look it. Come with me, Dr Wear will be waiting for us.'

'Can't you tell me what's happened? You said that it wasn't either of the girls. It's their mother?'

'Yes. It's not my job to say any more than that at this stage. This way.'

He followed the sister along a corridor and around two bends. In a separated room, they found Emily, apparently inert, brooded over by a young nurse and hooked up to a range of monitors and a drip. Emily was very white but her lips looked blue. Some sort of tent protected her body from the weight of bedclothes. A young policeman in uniform sat beside the bed with a notebook open on his knee and a pen in his hand, but Luke noticed that the page was blank.

'She hasn't said anything?' Luke asked him.

'Only to ask for Mr Grant. That would be yourself?' Luke nodded. 'She's heavily sedated but she might respond to your voice,' the constable said. 'That's what they told me. If so, ask her how it happened. We only know that she was found in the garage courtyard at Birchgrove. A vehicle seems to have crushed her.'

Luke paused for a moment to let his voice recover. 'I'll see what I can do.' He took a seat beside the head of the bed and picked up a limp hand. 'Emily?'

The still figure in the bed stirred, to the extent that it was not quite so totally motionless, and her eyes began to blink. 'GG?' she whispered. This was the nickname that his great-granddaughters had attached to him but she had never used it before.

He said, 'Yes.'

'Promise me,' she said, and stopped. Evidently speaking at all was very painful. 'Promise me you'll look after the girls.'

'Yes,' he said. 'Of course I will. If necessary and if there's nobody better suited...'

There was a moment of silence. He thought that she tried to shake her head. 'Promise,' she whispered. 'You're all there is.'

The constable was glaring at him in a meaning way. 'I promise. You didn't even have to ask. Can you tell us what happened to you?' he asked.

Again there was the faintest suggestion of a headshake. Her eyes closed and she seemed to drift away. The constable sighed. Luke spoke to her again but got no reaction.

Sister Macintyre beckoned with a bob of the head and led him back to the nurse's station. She spoke into a microphone and after a long minute a man in a white coat arrived. Luke had bumped into him occasionally at events over the years without learning his name or even that he was a doctor, but his lapel badge insisted that he was Doctor Wear. 'You'll want to know about your ... daughter?' he said.

'Granddaughter-in-law,' said Luke.

The doctor looked at him curiously and then resumed. 'She's badly injured, but no doubt you could see that for yourself. We don't have the facilities here to do much more than help her with transfusions and painkillers. As soon as she's strong enough, she'll be moved into Edinburgh for the highly skilled surgery that she needs.' The doctor looked solemn and his voice became decently hushed. 'That's if she lives. She has been badly crushed from the thorax to the pelvis. A broken leg has added to the shock, of course, but we've set and splinted that. That's about the level of surgery that we're equipped for. Two lower ribs are broken but they're still in place and I don't think they're threatening the lungs. The more serious damage...' The doctor went on to speak of ruptures and bruising to organs that Luke had never before been forced to try to envisage. Soon, his mind went blank.

When the doctor's voice came to a halt, Luke said, 'It's very bad, isn't it? When will you send her to Edinburgh?'

'The very moment that she's strong enough to travel. Tomorrow morning, perhaps.'

'Would she know me if I visited her again?

If she's strong enough.'

'Most unlikely. We let her float up towards the surface because she was fighting the painkillers and wouldn't settle until she'd seen you. In view of the damage, she's best kept heavily sedated. You may have to wait until she's undergone a series of major operations, but the New Royal in Edinburgh will advise you on that. And we haven't let her daughters see her at all.'

'I expect that that was sensible,' said Luke. 'Do you know where they are now?'

Doctor Wear half-smiled as he relaxed. The most difficult task for a doctor was over. 'They're in the Visitor's Waiting Room with a social worker. This way.'

Off another corridor, the Visitor's Waiting Room was behind a large sheet of glass. The room was well lit so that Luke saw his great-granddaughters before his presence registered. Somebody had taken pains to turn the room into a clever compromise between hospital efficiency and homelike comfort but the two girls, although reading separate and obviously inappropriate magazines, were sitting close on the settee and clearly depending on each other for support while the social worker watched benevolently. The scene was a study in mood, combining anxiety and suspense. He patted the miniature camera that was always in his shirt pocket but decided not to risk complicating the occasion any further.

The two girls looked up, undecided, as he entered. Then Jane, the younger, jumped up and ran to him, clasping him around the hips in a gesture of trust and affection that he found unexpected and vastly touching. He knew that he should have seen more of his great-granddaughters, but the effort of fending off his granddaughter-in-law's attempts to order him around had often been too great. On the occasions when he had met the girls there had undoubtedly been a bond, but Emily had remained firmly present as if to prevent any moral contamination. This he could understand without sympathizing.

'GG,' she said. 'Are we coming to stay with you? I'm sad,' she added.

He wanted to pick her up, but she was growing rapidly and his age and heart combined to make heavy lifting inadvisable. He detached her gently, led her to the settee and sat down between the two girls, putting an arm round each, but carefully in a manner that could not arouse suspicion in the most prurient-minded social worker. 'I'm not very happy either,' he said. 'As to you coming to live with me, at least until your mum's better, it seems rather likely and I'm quite happy about that. I've just promised your mother that I'll look after you. I have plenty of space. Perhaps you should go and have a walk in the garden, while we talk about it.'

The two girls exchanged a look. 'We'd rather stay and hear what you say,' said Violet.

He glanced at the social worker. She shrugged. 'All right,' he said. 'Just try not to interrupt unless there's something you don't understand. You can put your tuppence-worth in at the end. All right?'

They nodded solemnly.

Two

While he spoke with the girls, Luke's eyes had been straying to the social worker. He had a strong sense of *déjà vu*. His memory, jogged by the name on her lapel-badge, now began to throw up a recollection from long ago. He had first met Mariella Gilbert during Hannah's terminal illness. He had been surprised to receive a visit from a social worker rather than the usual health visitor but he assumed, without really thinking about it, that this was to check that he was coping well with looking after the pair of them. Only later did it occur to him that the purpose of the first visit might be to ensure that he was neither neglecting nor abusing his dying wife.

The social worker, a hard-faced older woman whose grey hair seemed to have been set in plastic, was on that occasion accompanied by a student. Mariella ('call me Ella') Gilbert was very young and very pretty in a blue-eyed, doll-like way but it was her figure – slender, broad-hipped and big breasted – that caught Luke's attention. She walked with an unconscious sway that lit a fire under his dreams. Luke himself was still in his twenties, just. His original masculine good looks (which, if he had been an actor, would have ensured him the lead in a swashbuckling bodice-ripper) were given a piratical embellishment by the eye-patch that he wore in preference to the rather uncomfortable artificial eye provided by the National Health Service and the scars remaining from the incident with the PIAT bomb. His remaining eye was drawn to the girl and from the frequency with which they made eye contact he was sure that she was equally provoked. He was a married man and, he told himself, faithful, but Hannah's enjoyment of sex had dwindled and then vanished. During the days that followed his meeting with Ella his mind returned to that figure and their mutual attraction as surely as his eye had been drawn to meet hers. The recurrent regret – *if only* – made a regular appearance even though he refused to recognize it. She was very young and, he thought, innocent.

On the next visit she came alone, explaining that the official social worker had a full caseload and since Mr Grant had obviously been coping so admirably with a very difficult situation it had been left to her to call and see that no fresh problems had arisen. It was spring but not very warm and he could see gooseflesh on her arms, but she had chosen to come in a thin and clinging dress that revealed every alluring undulation of firm young flesh. They pretended to ignore each other while they visited Hannah. Mariella helped with some of the attention required by the sick woman. Seeing the two together emphasized for him how Hannah had wasted. She was only beginning to recover the hair that she had lost to earlier chemotherapy. Her dependence still moved him towards tears.

But he was a young man, healthy and in need. As they returned downstairs, while he, in his innocence, was wondering whether a pass would be accepted or at least rejected in silence, Mariella stumbled. Luke, of course, attempted to catch her as a gentleman should, but somehow his grasp of her pliant body turned out, through no intent of his own, to be far from gentlemanly. The arm round her back arrived perilously close to a breast, but the other, which he had intended to support her knees, found a far more intimate clasp, which he was unable to change without dropping her. He carried her into the sitting room and laid her on the deep settee, where she recovered quickly. Her clothing had become somewhat disarranged but that seemed to perturb her very little. What followed was as inevitable as it was delicious.

When he had seen her to her car he returned upstairs. Hannah said, 'Did you have sex with her?'

Luke jumped and his tongue froze.

Hannah's chubbiness had fallen away during her illness and the bones of her skull were clearly visible. Even so, there was a trace of her old smile. 'You did, then? I could see that she was setting her cap at you. There were visible sparks jumping between you. It's all right,' she added quickly. 'I don't mind. I can't any more, as you know, and you must still have a need. I wouldn't want you to be walking around with a permanent hard-on. How could I grudge you a little relief when you're wearing yourself out and letting your own career go hang while you look after me, instead of letting me die in hospital? I know that you won't desert me.'

'Never,' he said. He felt ready to choke. Was ever a wife so generous?

'Never's a long time and I don't think I have that long, so I won't worry about it. Was she as good as me? Honest answer, please.'

He had to think about that. They had always been honest with each other. 'She was different,' he said at last. 'Not quite as good as you were in your prime. It didn't mean the same. You were always delicious. And inspired.'

'Don't overstate the case,' she said. She chuckled feebly. 'But I like to think so. We were good together, weren't we? Life hasn't gone on long enough. But when I look back, the very best moments were when we were together and I'm thankful for them. It's like that song. "When my life is through and the angels ask me to recall ... ".' Her voice was husky, but he knew the song.

He could only whisper. 'I will tell them I remember you.' He buried his face in the bedclothes rather than let her see him cry.

Most of the remaining visits that summer were paid by Mariella alone. Rather than let their affair come to Hannah's attention again, Luke smuggled some cushions out to the summerhouse. When her 'year out' ended and she had to return to college near Glasgow, they promised to write and they did indeed exchange several letters. Then Mariella met and married a fellow student and the correspondence lapsed.

And now, here she was again and with a wedding ring on her finger. She was severely and uninvitingly dressed but he thought that there was still a twinkle in her eye. It was not easy to know what to say to a lady who had been his mistress – good God! Was it really so many years ago? Her figure had thickened but only very slightly. The bone structure of her face was now blurred but her skin was still good, or did she have clever make-up to thank for that? He thought that retirement must be staring her in the face. 'We'll have to stop meeting like this,' he heard himself say. 'How does married life suit you?'

'Very well,' she said.

'How long have you been back in Newton

Lauder?'

Her eyes – still bright – looked away from his. His guess was that she felt guilty for being the inconstant one. 'A few months,' she said. 'We were facing cuts and my husband got a farm manager's job near here, so it's worked out quite well for us. Now to business,' she said briskly. 'These two are your granddaughters?'

'Great-granddaughters,' he said. He was tired of explaining. Sometimes he was tempted to accept the role of grandfather, at others he felt that to be great was great and a testament to family vigour and longevity.

'I suppose you could be a great-grandfather,' she said doubtfully.

'I married young and so did my daughter and her son. I'm eighty-one.'

'You don't look it.'

'Thank you. Nor do you.'

'I'm not,' she pointed out. 'You had quite a few years start on me.'

'Perhaps that explains it. But you should see the portrait in my attic.'

They laughed together.

'Even so, they retire me soon.' She became serious. 'Could you undertake responsibility for these two?'

It was a moment for decision. He could see his peaceful routine being blown away. No more dozing in front of the television. It would be the Pops and staying up late to see them safely home. But when he looked at them, they were regarding him anxiously. And what else was to become of them? He felt a surge of love. 'I think so,' he said. 'Until their mother's fit again. Unless somebody more suitable comes forward, but there's nobody on my side nearer than California and I don't think that any of her very few relatives were still speaking to her. She has a knack of putting people's backs up. But I'm very fond of the girls. I still live in the same house and there's room.'

'She did specifically want them in your care.'

'I don't know why. We didn't even like each other very much. I haven't even seen them all that often. She didn't approve of me.' He glanced at the girls but neither seemed surprised. 'Perhaps, like she said, I'm all there is,' he said.

'She always says that you're a clever devil, GG,' said Jane.

The older sibling decided that the ice had been broken. 'She said that you had charm but you didn't use it very wisely. Well, that's what she *said*.'

'I think she may have been right,' Luke said. 'Some day, you can tell me what you think.'

Mariella nodded in spite of herself. 'Why do they call you GG?' she asked.

'They found great-granddad rather a mouthful. It became GGD, but that's just as many syllables so it got shortened to GG.'

'I see. It makes you sound like a horse.' She turned to the girls. 'Do you want to stay with your ... *great*-grandfather?'

Again the two girls exchanged a look. They both nodded. 'But don't call my great-granddad a horse,' said Jane.

Mariella smiled. 'Go with God and your great-grandfather,' she said. 'He managed to cope single-handed with your great-grandmother's last illness, so he should be able to cope with you two. But try to pull your weights. He's not as young as he used to be.'

'He's not old,' Jane said. 'He's just the age that he is, that's all.'

'I understand,' said Mariella.

The town of Newton Lauder sits in a valley

below one of the main roads southwards from Edinburgh. The town itself is limited in size. It is surrounded by good agricultural land; just the sort of land, in fact, to which planners are inclined to direct new developments. But the town is also fringed by beds and outcrops of the local stone, unprofitable to farm but excellent for building.

An old road climbed eastward from the town, with a hairpin bend to ease the climb for the occasional horse and cart and to avoid a steep climb to a rocky plateau. A site above the hairpin had been available when the hospital was built. Luke's home was on a farm road that came off the hairpin and gave access to some scattered farms. Those parts of the land least susceptible to cultivation had been abandoned and soon returned to birch woodland and heather.

Luke's house, substantially built of the local stone, had been constructed to house the family of a farmer who had abandoned the effort to scratch a living from the rock and had moved further north. The site was good. The main rooms looked north and had a view across the valley, over the roofs of Newton Lauder to the sunlit hills beyond. The other rooms faced south across a

31

lawn to where a row of beech trees provided shelter from the prevailing wind and shade in summer but allowed the sunlight to filter across the lawn when the leaves were down. There were no very near neighbours.

The building of the hospital had brought mains water, drainage and other services into the area, and it had not been long before a local builder had seen his chance and developed the small plateau within the loop of the hairpin. He had built thirty houses around a garage court in a so-called 'Radburn' layout (after Radburn, New Jersey) in which pedestrian and vehicle traffic were carefully segregated. The area was known as Birchgrove after a feature that had been removed to make room for it.

Vehicle access was properly from the upper road, but arriving there from the town entailed a long detour and a very sharp and rather blind bend. Access could be obtained more directly from the direction of the town by way of a rough and precipitous track rising from the lower leg of the road. This was too steep and rough for anything but a Land Rover to negotiate. However, the son of the local garage-owner had his own business restoring and reselling

Land Rovers. In the largely agricultural Borders he did good business. Olive-green Land Rovers were the vehicle of choice in the area.

Ella Gilbert was overdue at another appointment and was pleased to release the girls into the custody of their great-grandfather. Luke shook her hand with special warmth on parting, for she had first introduced him to the delights to be found away from the paths of virtue. Without her he might have settled into a lifetime as a celibate widower, eternally respecting the memory of his late wife. He collected the cluttered ring of keys that Emily had had in her pocket and they walked out into the sunshine in silence, all overawed by the changes coming over them.

Pepper was not so impressed. Always a very sociable bitch, she had encountered the girls several times in the past and with a Labrador's voracity for food she remembered them as a soft touch for titbits. Her rapturous welcome broke the ice and the half-mile journey passed with the girls twisted round in the rear seats to renew their acquaintance with the yellow bitch. She knew better than to climb over from her place behind the seats. Luke recognized the first major change to his life. There had not been a passenger in his Land Rover for almost as long as he could remember. It had been a solitary life, but that was over.

Luke drove back to the road and turned down the hill. The girls returned their attention to him when he turned off onto the loop road round Birchgrove and pulled up at Cayley.

'Are you coming to live with us?' Jane demanded.

'You'll have to come to live with me,' Luke explained. 'All my things are there and that includes the way I make my living. Also, my house is larger and anyway I don't like people looking at me over the garden fence. You'll need to collect whatever you want. Just for a night or two. We can come back.'

'That's all right,' Violet said. 'I think we always felt a bit cramped here. We love your house. And there's room for Jane to run around outside without always being told to be careful of the traffic.'

Luke had his reservations about that but there would be time enough later to worry about misconceptions. He could see quite enough scope for friction already. When the time came to say 'go to bed' or 'get ready for school' would they do it? And, if not, what action would he take? Life was about to become complicated.

He knew from previous visits that there was a substantial table in their hall. 'All right,' he said as they entered. 'Bags or cases on the hall table and put there what you want to take with you. Essentials first. Like I said, we can always come back.'

He waited in the hall while they pattered or, in Jane's case, thundered up and down the stairs. He let his mind stray to the changes that would be necessary to his regime. But soon he was trying to enforce a little moderation on the packing. Jane, as he suspected, was determined to bring a large collection of soft toys and she seemed totally uninterested in pyjamas, changes of clothing or toothbrushes. Violet, at first glance, seemed more sensible. He decided to overlook a small stack of romantic magazines. She had provided herself with rather more pharmaceuticals than he would have believed necessary. This impelled him to take a closer look. Surely at her age and with her skin a full complement of cosmetics was not called for. He had thought at first that she had tucked underwear at the bottom of the stack of clothes out of modesty, which he appreciated. But then he noticed a fringe of lace that was surely not appropriate for a teenager.

'Let's have an agreement,' he said. 'No lies between us, ever. Always the truth. All right?'

They nodded. 'If you insist,' said Violet.

'I do. Now please separate out your mother's clothes and make-up for putting back. This isn't the right occasion for helping yourself.'

Violet made a face. 'She lets me borrow things.'

Luke pushed a hand into the pile and pulled out a pair of panties which Luke would have considered too daring even for Emily, let alone her daughters. 'What's she going to think when she comes back and finds that you've pinched all her most...' He broke off while he searched for the right word. 'Her most grown-up clothes and make-up?'

Violet had turned pink. She had been making a secret face at him but he was slow on the uptake. She was forced to speak up.

'Mum *is* coming back, then?'

Jane was nearby. She turned and faced into the corner.

While he hesitated, Violet added, 'No lies between us, ever. Remember? When I asked about that, they gave the sort of answer that they'd have given whether she was only having her toenails clipped or if she was already...'

'I remember,' he said. She had backed him into a corner. 'I won't lie to you. I just don't know. I haven't had a chance to speak to the doctors yet and they probably won't know until they've done all the tests. She spoke to me weakly but quite sensibly.'

He had more to say but he was brought to a halt by the realization that Jane was quietly sobbing into a well-used handkerchief. He might have coped with howls but this quiet misery was more difficult. And he had promised to be truthful. He put an arm round her and gave her a cleaner handkerchief. 'I can't tell you anything,' he said, 'but I'll find out when I can. She was alive and speaking when I saw her. And there's an old saying that while there's life there's hope. Just remember that your lives are going on and we'll try to make them as good as we can. And now, that's enough on that subject. When I left home this morning I had no idea that I was to expect two young ladies as guests. Let's get your luggage sorted out. You want pyjamas or nighties, whatever you use at bedtime and a change of clothes for tomorrow. What about school?'

'We just broke up for the summer,' Violet said.

Was that good or bad? He would be spared the problems of getting them off to school on time with all the right accoutrements. On the other hand, they would be under his feet all day unless he could organize. 'You can bring a few of your favourite things but you'll have to give me a chance to get ready for you. We'll drop those things off at my house and then we'll have to go down to the shops. You'll have to tell me which are your favourite foods.'

'Mum's freezer is probably full,' Violet said.

'That's a good thought. She certainly won't be back tomorrow or the next day and there's no point letting good food go bad. Show me where she keeps it and find me a couple of cardboard cartons. Jane, let's go and wash your face in cold water and then let's see you smile.'

Anxiety was still present but the removal turned into quite a jolly party.

Three

Luke was a creature of habit and his habit was to be early to bed and early to rise. In this, he was not following a precept often advocated during his youth nor was he as his friends supposed trying to catch the soft, early morning light that was so ideal for photography. It was simply because his well-being was conditioned by his sleep and he liked to awake of his own accord. A habit of later rising made those occasions when he was forced to submit to the tyranny of the alarm clock, to meet a client or to catch a plane, such abject misery. This had suited the girls, who were exhausted by the traumas of a day that had begun with the absence of a mother who was *always* there. Jane trotted off to bed obediently at the first asking and Violet followed not long afterwards.

Luke woke next morning at his usual time.

But it soon came to him that the times were going to be far from usual. He was going to have to face up to noise and inconvenience. He was used to awaking in a house that was silent except for the sound of the central heating boiler, but he remembered from the distant past the shouts and crashes as a young family prepared to face the day. There was none of the expected hullabaloo. Why not? Had they died in the night? Run away to sea? Been kidnapped? Or were they still in deep sleep? But he realized that he could hear faintly the sound of movements and hushed voices. He rolled out of bed and then checked himself. He was accustomed to sleeping in an old T-shirt but that would never do before his great-granddaughters. The habit of years had moulded his morning movements into a streamlined flow that no time-and-motion study could have improved. The time that it took for the kettle to boil, for instance, was exactly how long it took to let Pepper out, lay the table and prepare the dog's breakfast. But today, Pepper was going to have to wait. He made a mental note to buy a dressing gown. Luckily he had a shower room *en suite* so that he could be decently shaved and dressed before confronting the girls.

He need not have been quite so fastidious. When he arrived downstairs, in slippers but otherwise dressed, the dishes placed neatly beside the sink and the mess sprinkled over the table indicated that the girls had breakfasted on cereal and milk. The outside door stood wide open but Pepper had resisted the temptation to join in the game that was afoot on the lawn outside. It was Luke's habit to feed her twice a day rather than give her one large meal which he believed, stretched her stomach and therefore increased her appetite. She greeted him as usual and presented him with her favourite toy, a teddy bear with the stuffing threatening to emerge, and then made it clear that she was waiting for her breakfast.

Luke sighed. He rather thought that he might be doing a lot of sighing over the coming weeks. On the previous day, they had lunched in a small but good café just off the Square in Newton Lauder and the girls' table manners had been impeccable. Encouraged by this sign that Emily's teaching had not all been in vain, and to evade the difficulty of knowing what on earth to talk about with two girls sixty-odd years younger than himself, he had tried to impress on them that he expected, or at the very least hoped, that they would clear up behind themselves.

A friend had once grumbled to him that allowing two children to share a bedroom led only to tears, and not only on the part of the children, because the recurrent theme soon became 'I didn't drop it so I'm not going to pick it up.' He had therefore allocated them a bedroom apiece. The result, he saw from a quick glance through the wide open doors, was that he now had two bedrooms, each resembling an explosion in a Chinese laundry, instead of only one. He had expected no better from Jane but Violet, being the elder, should have set an example, or so he told himself. On the other hand, they had been remarkably considerate about letting him sleep.

Their arrival at his home, Whinmount, had been the occasion for him to point out that Pepper had not been walked and he persuaded the two girls to undertake this errand along a track that branched off his access road. This gave him his only chance for a hasty search through the house for such souvenirs as his lady guests might have left behind over the years. As he had allowed his clientele to dwindle he had been left with a few bedrock clients, in particular a publisher whose preference in dust jackets ran to glamour photographs, and only Luke Grant's photographs were sufficiently glamorous without quite passing over the boundary into soft porn. The publisher wanted dust jackets that would attract a man to lift the book but not so raunchy that he would have to hide it from his wife. Luke had that knack. Hastily he filed away some prints and the scripts of another batch from which he was to select the incidents to be illustrated. He moved on to the rest of the house. Absolute truth was all very well but there was no need to tarnish the saintly image held, he hoped, by his two great-granddaughters. A phone call caught him with one diaphanous nylon stocking in his hand. But where on earth was the other? Surely none of his guests could unwittingly have gone home half-hosed! He rolled up the dainty souvenir and transferred it into a rubbish bin.

The phone call was from the police. Inspector Fellowes would call on him in about two hours' time. Luke made one call to the hospital and then set about his own break-fast and the kitchen. By the time that all was clean and orderly, Jane had tired of their game on the lawn and Violet was tired of trying to keep her amused. They arrived in the doorway and looked at him hopefully.

'First things first,' he said. 'This is Sunday. Would your mother want you to attend church?'

'Lord no!' Violet said. 'She thinks that the whole idea of God as a person is daffy. She says that He was invented by men to enslave women. Why do people believe in God?'

Luke managed not to pull a face. 'I'll try to explain some time when we have several hours to spare. For the moment, take it as a combination of wishful thinking and a simple way to tell primitive people to be good. I'm expecting a visitor later, but we have time to walk Pepper and do something useful. Then you can tidy your rooms.'

He chivvied Jane into brushing her tangled chestnut hair and both of them into putting on sensible shoes while he did the same. The two girls were both going to resemble their mother and Emily, for all her faults, was a looker. While they walked, with Pepper investigating all the interesting scents of the new day, he said, 'I've phoned the hospital. Your mother came through the night well. She's got over the shock and she's a little stronger so they're sending her in to Edinburgh this morning. They'll probably operate on her later today. To make her better,' he explained to Jane.

'They *will* make her better?' Jane asked.

'We have a bargain. Only the truth. Darling, I don't know. We'll probably know more by tonight after a scan and a beginning to operations. Meantime, we only know that they're keeping her comfortable and doing their best for her.'

They turned off the farm track and came out on a grassy area among scattered gorse bushes. A view over the town opened up. Pheasants, most of them not yet quite fully-grown, scattered in front of them. Pepper looked up at him expectantly. 'The reason that I come this way in the mornings,' he said, 'is that I have an agreement with Mr Calder. You know him?'

Jane nodded. 'At the skateboard shop.'

'And fishing rods,' said Violet.

Keith Calder's main business was with shotguns but Luke let that go by for the moment. 'I have an arrangement with Mr

Calder,' he said. 'He runs the shoot here. It's in two halves split by a Forestry Commission bit – all those dark-looking plantations on the rise there. He's a busy man and it's a big help to him if I do the dogging-in on this half. Any dog needs walking, regularly.'

'What's dogging-in?' Violet asked.

'Pheasants can wander off. They never know where home is. They always think that there must be something better over the next hill and they never find their way back. You can't fence them in once they can fly. The best you can do is to go round the boundaries in the morning and send them back towards their home coverts before they wander too far. We go this way.'

They angled down the slope to the fence line. Luke gave Pepper a nod and the bitch entered a patch of rough ground. Several pheasants whirred into the air, the cocks chortling indignantly, and headed for home. 'GG,' Jane said, 'do you shoot?'

'No. I'll go on being honest,' Luke said. 'I would if I could. I did shoot a lot while I was young and I was quite good at it. But now I can't see out of my right eye and I never learned to shoot off my left shoulder. There are lots of other ways to manage, but none of them work for me.'

'Mum said that shooting's cruel.'

That was exactly what he would have expected her to say. 'She lets you eat chicken?' he asked.

'Yes.'

'Well, some day I'll take you to see where they raise chickens and how they transport them and kill them when they're big enough. Then you can ask yourselves whether you'd rather be one of those chickens or a pheasant that was put out on the ground not long ago and will have to take its chance over the guns sometimes during November, December and January, with about a fifty-fifty chance of being left to live, die or even breed in the wild. You can make your own minds up then whether you want to come with me in the mornings and perhaps even come beating and be paid for it when the season starts. I'll tell you all about that later.'

They followed the boundary. Soon, Luke judged that Jane was tiring. His own legs were wearied – he was not as fleet as he had been. But they had covered the vulnerable stretch of the boundary. Along the remainder, there was little feed and no cover to tempt the pheasants over the fence. They turned back. Along the way, he pointed out and named trees, wildflowers, birds and animals and showed them how you could tell one animal from the other by their footprints and droppings. Both girls began to chatter with intelligent questions. He decided that conversation was not going to be so difficult after all.

Coffee for two and biscuits and milk for one. Violet considered herself to be adult except when it suited her to claim the privileges of childhood. When he heard the approaching vehicle he said, 'The time has arrived for you to tidy your bedrooms. Violet, please help Jane. Now go.'

'Must we?'

'We're being honest, remember? I would not have said it if I didn't mean it.'

With much sighing and dragging of footsteps, the two girls set off upstairs.

Four

Generalizations are usually subject to more than a little blurring at the edges. Nevertheless, at some time in history it must have been possible to draw a line across Scotland, roughly north-east to south-west, separating the area where the thin and dark Highlanders predominated from where the more thickset and sandy-haired Lowlanders reigned. Time and migration have blurred that line but Inspector Ian Fellowes – Detective Inspector Ian Fellowes, Luke noted – was definitely of the Lowlands. He was wearing a light tweed jacket and a kilt.

They had in fact met before. Luke was surprised to recognize the younger man who had opposed and bested him at darts in the Canal Bar earlier that year. He took the inspector into his sitting room, gave him a chair, left him for a minute while he fetched more coffee and then settled down opposite.

They exchanged brief comments on the weather while the inspector glanced around the bright, worn but comfortable room.

The inspector produced a small tape recorder and placed it on the low table between them. 'I'm very short-handed at the moment,' he said. 'And busy. Break-ins in three different villages, an attempted fraud at a post office, shoplifting in a super-market, a pub fight and an attempted black-mail. Those are definite crimes. This one may turn out to have been an accident. It is even possible that the driver didn't know that he'd hit anybody. So I'm doing these interviews on my own. You won't mind if I get it on tape? I can concentrate better if I don't have to take notes. Mrs Highsmith is your daughter? Or daughter-in-law?'

'She's my granddaughter-in-law. To save you asking, I'm eighty-one. My family has a tradition of procreating early in life. What can you tell me about her accident? At the hospital they could only say that she seemed to have been crushed by a vehicle.'

'I'll tell you what I can,' said Fellowes. 'But first, let's follow procedures and have you answer a few questions before my informa-tion gives you a lead.'

'That seems reasonable. But first of all, let me ask how it happens that a detective inspector is dealing with what I thought was a traffic accident.'

The DI studied Luke for a moment. 'That's something else that we'll come back to,' he said. 'Tell me about your grand-daughter-in-law. How do you get on with her?'

So somebody was dissatisfied with the accident theory. Luke decided that whatever he held back at this stage might be counted against him later. 'We do not get on. I warned my grandson not to marry her and I believe she knew it and held it against me; but we were never destined to be friends. I could have forgiven her for being bossy except that I disagreed with almost every word that she said. I suppose she felt much the same about me. Henry went ahead any-way. He only had to put up with her for about ten years – then he was killed in a plane crash. He seems to have left her ade-quately provided for. I see her as arrogant and opinionated and I'm relieved to find that she hasn't irredeemably stamped her opinions on my great-granddaughters.' Luke shrugged. 'She probably has certain opinions about me and she may be right. She's entitled to her views and I know that I can be a pig-headed old man. The difference was that I was always right and she was wrong.'

Fellowes had seemed rather stiff and formal but now laughter lines creased the corners of his eyes. 'What in particular might have given rise to her opinion of you?'

'That's for me to know and for you to find out,' Luke said. 'Not many people can see themselves clearly enough to answer such a question. And, once again to save you asking, I took a lady to dinner at the Ballintree Bistro in Newton Lauder on Friday evening. After dinner she came back here with me and we watched a video for a couple of hours. She had left her car here so she drove herself home and I went straight to bed just after midnight – which is very late by my standards – so I think I can satisfy you that I didn't run any lady over. The first that I knew of any accident was when the hospital phoned me in the morning.'

'Who was the lady you took to dinner?'

Luke thought for a moment before he replied. But the facts were bound to come out. At the recollection of that evening something stirred in him but, sadly, it did not reach his loins. 'Helena Harper,' he said. 'Of Menu, Birchgrove.'

'I know of her.' The detective inspector paused and frowned. 'Menu seems an odd name for a house.'

'Me-and-you,' Luke explained. 'Somebody's idea of a sentimental joke.'

'Ah. It was Mrs Harper who found Mrs Highsmith. About eleven fifty, that was. She got in a bit of a state.'

'She does that sometimes.'

'She did it this time all right.' Inspector Fellowes laughed shortly. 'She scooted home, dialled nine-nine-nine to report finding Mrs Highsmith and then phoned her sister. Her sister lives about twenty minutes away, and by the time she got to Mrs Harper's house she found her in an advanced state of hysteria. This was before we arrived.' DI Fellowes sounded rather relieved. 'The sister had called for an ambulance. It was the medics who called us. When we got there, the injured woman had been removed, Mrs Harper's sister had already put her to bed with a hot toddy and a sleeping pill and we haven't had a chance to speak to her because she says that she wants you to be present. Why would that be?'

'Moral support, probably. Shall I phone her?'

At the inspector's nod, Luke picked up his mobile phone. Helena answered, so her sister must have returned to her husband and family. The phone had remarkable volume for its size. He held it slightly away from his ear so that the DI could hear what Helena said. 'You're getting over the shock from your grisly find of last night?' he asked.

'You've heard, then?' Her voice was unsteady.

'I could hardly not. She's my granddaughter-in-law.'

'Is that who it was? I didn't stop to take a look and the light was bad anyway. Is she ... how is she?'

'Being taken into Edinburgh for scanning and surgery, the last I heard. I'm afraid it doesn't sound too good. Listen, I have the local police inspector here. The *detective* inspector. He wants a word with you as the finder of the ... the victim, but you said that you wanted me to be present. We'd come to you, only I have my great-granddaughters with me and I think it's too early to leave them to their own devices. They don't know their way around here, where not to go and that sort of thing. Can you come to me?'

'I suppose so. I'm a bit shaky but I'm fit to drive. I wouldn't want to end up in the stream again.'

Her words had brought it all back to him. He toyed with his memories while he waited and Inspector Fellowes transcribed notes from the taped record.

About two and a half years earlier, Luke had been relaxing in front of a log fire. He was already in his sleeping T-shirt and slippers but, not feeling sleepy, he was sipping a final brandy and watching some television. It was Pepper who suddenly roused and went to the door. Luke had learned to read the bitch's body language and he could tell that she knew something was wrong. He went to the front door and opened it against the chain. Snow had been falling in occasional light showers but from the ridge on the doorstep he could tell that there had been a heavier fall.

He could also hear what had disturbed Pepper. A woman's voice was screaming for help.

The snow seemed to have stopped but he

was not going out in his T-shirt and slippers. He threw on his sheepskin coat and pushed his feet into wellingtons. He sent Pepper to her bed. One of his biggest hates was drying a wet dog. The snow came halfway up his wellingtons, making walking hard work. A bitter wind blew up the skirt of his sheepskin coat.

Lights and the screams drew him along the approach road. Snow had stopped and there was a bright moon. There were tyre-tracks in the snow, partly blurred by the last of the snowfall. It was soon obvious what had happened. A driver, heading back towards the B-road and probably blinded by the falling snow, had become disoriented, tried to brake, skidded wildly and run over the brink, down into the stream. This was still swollen by the brief thaw that had preceded the latest fall of snow. It was narrow but deep and the arrival of a Land Rover had almost blocked it, causing the water to rise above the level of the bonnet.

With the utmost reluctance, Luke discarded his sheepskin at the waterside and slithered down the bank. The chill was lethal but he had to do what he could. Cautiously, while leaning hard against the flow, he managed the few steps to the Land Rover, and clung on for dear life to one of the door mirrors before the water could sweep him away. The window was partially open but it was jammed in that position. The door, too, was hopelessly stuck. The door on the other side was resting against a tree-root. The woman, still screaming, was holding out her hands to him – a gesture of only symbolic significance. The water was up to her chest but showed no sign of rising higher.

'I'll be back in a minute or two,' he shouted above the rush of the water. He made the bank in one leap, grabbed at a small bush and with its help hauled himself up to road level. He recovered his sheepskin and set off back to his house, jogging uncomfortably in his waterlogged wellingtons while struggling back into his sheepskin. Bitterly cold water squeezed between his toes and squirted up his legs. His behaviour, he knew, was absolute insanity in one with a heart attack only a few years behind him but he had to balance the possibility of another and this time fatal heart attack to himself against the virtual certainly of a miserable death for another human being. But the woman was younger than he and therefore had more life at stake.

Luckily, he knew exactly where his crowbar was because he had used it only that day to shift a log. He grabbed it up and started back. It was agony to jettison his coat and re-enter the freezing water. The woman was still screaming but as hoarseness overcame her the noise grated less. He had to hold on with one hand and ply the crowbar with the other, but he managed to get a purchase and whatever gripped the door came free so suddenly that he almost lost his footing. He dragged the door open and the power of the water slammed it all the way and held it there.

He needed a moment to think out the next move but the woman wanted nothing more than to get out of the vehicle. She kicked off from the further door and managed to grasp Luke around the neck. Only his grip on the doorpost saved them both from being swept away. Looking frantically around he saw that the bush that he had used earlier was within reach but too flimsy for the double load. Just behind it, however, was a stout birch sapling. He reversed his grip on his crowbar and, holding it by the chisel end, managed to hook the sapling with the other.

The drag on his freezing fingers against the smooth metal was insupportable but he clung on for both their lives and the current swung them round and thumped them against the bank.

At some point the woman had stopped screaming though he had been unaware of it. Now she released her clasp on his neck and kicked herself upwards, largely against him. She rolled onto the narrow strip of bank between the road and the stream and seemed to pass out although he could see that her body was racked with shivering.

He was almost done but he managed to haul himself up beside her, abandoning his crowbar. They were both in great danger from hypothermia. One more effort, he told himself. He was almost eighty but he had kept himself very fit until his heart attack and fortunately she was a featherweight. He resumed his sheepskin coat again but left it open. When he lifted her in his arms, cradled like a baby, he tried at the same time to pull the coat around them both. He could not be sure that she had gained any benefit from the coat and he had certainly allowed bitterly cold air to circulate around his own limbs, but a sort of inhibition restrained him from recovering her share of his coat. He set off back to the house. His boots had metal studs or he could never have kept his feet. It seemed a mile to his front door and his arms were on the point of failing him by the time he pushed it open. He closed it with his bottom, carried her into the still warm sitting room and dumped her none too gently on the settee.

He could think of all the things that he had to do, but in what order? He let instinct take over. Another log on the fire, dash into the kitchen and put the kettle on, restart the central heating and return. With some difficulty he kicked his wellingtons off in the hall and poured the water into the toilet beside the door. His sheepskin had become thoroughly wet and was doing him no good so he dragged it off and draped it over the hall radiator.

Back in the sitting room, the woman was crouched in front of the fire. Like him, she had found that wet clothes did no more than protect her from the warmth of the fire and draw away by the cool of evaporation what warmth the body had. Luke's teeth were chattering loudly. He decided that this was no time for modesty. He crouched beside her, luxuriating in the heat radiating from the glowing logs, and dragged off his T-shirt. The woman had already reduced herself to nudity. She was still shivering violently but her hysteria had abated and she seemed to be lapsing into a trance.

His heart was still thumping and he could feel the cramping in his left arm that sometimes presaged a heart attack. A call to the emergency services was undoubtedly called for but he considered the sum asked for bringing a phone line to the house to be beyond all reason. He had depended on his mobile but this had been in the pocket of his sheepskin and was now lost under either water or snow.

The heat was drying them off, but he made a quick dash to the airing cupboard and fetched several warm, dry bath-towels. On the way, he found his nitrolingual spray and gave himself a spray on his tongue. He joined her again on the hearthrug. His own thinning hair took only a minute, but he gave the woman a circulation-restoring rub and then wrapped her hair in a towel. She submitted like a child. He was seeing her as a person for the first time rather than a subject for rescue. She was past her first youth but she had retained a trim figure. Her face showed signs of the passing years, but not enough to detract from a cast of features that suggested kindness, humour and a capacity for affection. It might never have been beautiful but hers was the sort of face that improved with keeping as happiness made a stronger imprint than time.

He had also fetched the brandy bottle and some lemonade to dilute the sting. She sipped gladly and it put new warmth into her.

Her shivering subsided into an occasional spasm but her eyes had still not come back into focus. It was for no more need than a hug and an exchange of body warmth that she turned to him.

It is a cruel jest of fate that a man may lose the physical ability for love while the desire is still paramount. If he has a partner who will share alternative sex with him he is lucky, because sheer embarrassment makes the courting of a new partner a matter of great difficulty.

Luke had not been in a relationship when dysfunction overtook him. For several years the need for physical release had not been a necessity but merely a comfort when it happened. However, he still missed the romance, the glamour, the exchange of loving. It was with a renewed sadness that he realized that the contact with a naked and attractive woman, however pleasing emotionally, did nothing for him physically. Even when, moving like an automaton, she put a hand down to him, he did not stir. Physically, he could tell that she was very much aroused.

Later, she explained that Luke had arrived in her moment of despair, had shared her danger and agony, had carried her in his arms and brought her to safety, warmth and comfort. The distress that the effort had caused him had been obvious but he had struggled and overcome it. To her, he had become a heroic figure, entitled to heroic rewards. The brandy, she admitted, might also have played a part. She had reached a point at which nothing was too much to offer her gallant saviour. When he released himself and turned to put another log on the fire, he was accessible and she lowered her mouth to him. The ominous grumbling in his chest and left arm had subsided. It was a moment of high emotion. One minute later they were indulging in the passion that has no name but only a two-digit number.

On that occasion, she stayed for a week but returned to her own house in Birchgrove when her cousin was due to come for a visit. Their episodes became a regular feature of their lives but they had never quite arrived at a state for commitment. A more or less secret romance pleased them both. It offered both glamour and physical release without much need to adapt to each other's whims about the housekeeping.

An unmistakably Land Rover noise announced the arrival of Helena. Luke hoisted himself to his feet in order to let her in but the detective inspector got there first and opened the door to her. Looking Luke squarely in the eye he said, 'I'm sure that Mrs Harper would like a cup of tea.'

'Oh, I would!' Helena said. 'You wouldn't mind, Luke?'

Luke could take a hint with the best of them. But first he took a careful look beyond Helena. Her spaniel did not get on with Pepper. 'Shaun isn't with you?'

'He died quite suddenly on Thursday and I buried him in his favourite place in the garden.' Her voice was husky. 'You remember, Luke? Under the clump of buddleia, where he could be in shade or sheltered, whichever he liked. I think he'd picked up some poison that the council had put down for rats.' Her voice ended with a sob.

'I'm sorry,' he said. 'I know how much he meant to you. When you've got over it, we'll think about a puppy for you. It's the best way.'

He retreated to the kitchen. Both doors closed, presumably by the inspector's hand, but the sitting room had originally been a dining room and a serving hatch had only been papered over. He could hear every word as the inspector offered Helena a seat. Then, 'Mrs Harper, what did you do on Friday evening before finding Mrs Highsmith?'

'Mr Grant took me to dinner at that Bistro place just outside the Square on the road back towards Edinburgh. Then we came back here and watched a film. *Weekend at Bernie's*. Luke has it on video. He'd watched it before but he said that he didn't mind seeing it again. It's very funny, we both thought.'

And that, Luke thought, should satisfy the

inspector that we aren't cooking up alibis between us. No doubt the inspector would check up on the telephone records. The kettle, which had still been hot, returned to the boil quickly and without undue noise and he made tea. As he carried the tray into the sitting room Helena was trying to explain the plot of the film. She thanked him for the tea. Nobody hinted that he should go away again so Luke resumed his seat.

'And after the video finished,' said Inspector Fellowes. 'What then?'

Helena was not one of nature's liars. Nor was she unduly secretive. She would have been quite capable of saying, 'After that we had a lovely romp on the hearthrug and then I went home.' Instead she said 'We talked.' But her face was bright pink. 'I left for home at about eleven forty. Twenty to twelve,' she added in case the inspector's arithmetic let him down. 'It must have been about then because when Luke switched off his telly the programme that was just starting was the one that was advertised to start at that time.' She was improvising but doing it, Luke thought, quite well although perhaps elaborating too much. DI Fellowes would probably see through her but he would see that she was only defending her own reputation. As for Luke, he was unconcerned for himself. His reputation had blown away on the wind fifty years earlier.

'Go on, please.'

'Well, all right. I drove back towards Birchgrove. I turned left towards the hospital.'

'Is that usual? I thought you Birchgrove residents all used the steep track from the other side.'

'We do,' Helena said. 'Ordinarily. If we're coming from the town. But I was already higher up than that. I was hardly going to go down the hill in order to come up again by a steep and stony track, now was I, Inspector?'

'I suppose not. Go on.'

'So I came in by the proper road from near the hospital entrance. If you want the exact time, I had the car radio on and they were playing Gershwin's *Walking The Dog* on Classic FM. Such a happy tune, I always think, and often very appropriate. Then ... I suppose you want to know about the other car?'

Her two listeners, who had been lulled by her gentle voice, snapped into alertness.

'Other car?' said the inspector.

'Yes. I'll tell you. I expect you know the layout.' But she went on to expound it. 'You come from here and turn up towards the hospital, or down the proper road if you're coming from the direction of the hospital. Coming from here, you turn off to your right into Birchgrove. Almost immediately you have the garage court on your left just before the private road becomes very rough and dives down towards the town. Inside the court you have a row of garages each side and at the end there's a gap for a path each side. And then there's a brick wall across the end with ivy and Virginia creeper planted outside. Inside it's bare brick, but rather a nice brick, all browns and purples.

'There's no lighting in the garage court. Well, after all, cars are expected to have lights on. There are streetlights outside but though their light shines into the courtyard they leave a dark space at the wall and that's where she was. I'd just put my car away and I was walking to my house. I don't know how I'd missed seeing her in the car's lights except that I was concentrating on picking out my lock-up to stop at. Then I nearly missed seeing her again because there's so little light. I think I only found her at all because I heard a small sound and my foot kicked against something that had fallen out of her shopping. My car key has a little battery and a bulb in it. There isn't much light but it was just enough to show me the ... the...' She broke off with a shudder.

'Don't distress yourself,' Inspector Fellowes said. He sounded as though for two pins he would have patted her hand. Helena was a very feminine woman and she had that effect on men. 'You were going to tell us about the other car.'

'So I was. Let me think.' She thought. 'After I'd turned off the other road, the *proper* road, I could see the entry to the garage court about fifty or sixty yards in front of me and to my left. The lights of a car shone out of the entry and then a car came out and turned away from me. It disappeared over the hump but I could see its lights shining on the trees and bouncing as it went down the track. It seemed to be hurrying.'

'Did it indeed? Have you any idea what sort of a car it was?'

'Oh yes. It was a Land Rover just like mine.'

Luke decided to join the party. He picked

up the tea tray. 'That won't help you very much, Inspector,' he said. 'Most of the ladies up here have them and two-car families usually have one as a second car. There are still a lot of unsurfaced roads around here and with a Land Rover you can take a very useful short cut up the hill. Young Ledbetter makes his living buying them up, restoring them and putting them back into circulation. The Land Rover is still suited to that sort of treatment. If a part's worn out, you just unbolt it and bolt on a new one. It isn't as simple as it used to be, but it's still true. You don't need all the specialized machinery that most of the modern cars need.'

'You didn't happen to notice which model of Land Rover it was? No?'

'I didn't even know that there were different models,' Helena said. 'They all look the same to me, the boxy ones, up until they went all classy and expensive with the Discovery and that sort. More like cars than jeeps.'

'So it could even have been one of the foreign copies?'

'I suppose so. But I think it was one of the older ones like mine, like a biscuit tin on wheels. The foreign ones don't usually look like that.'

The inspector sighed. Evidently he was not accustomed to witnesses so totally un-observant about vehicles. 'Could you be sure of the colour by night?'

'No ... No, I couldn't. I think it was all one colour and dark, but whether it was the usual olive green I couldn't say. But I did see the driver.'

Ian Fellowes had resigned himself to getting no more from this witness. In his sudden excitement he raised his voice. 'Whooo...' The sound emerged like a fog-horn. 'I do beg your pardon.' He lowered his voice. 'Who was it?'

'I don't know.'

The inspector closed his eyes for a moment. 'You don't?'

Her voice took on the tone of somebody explaining something very simple. 'It was dark, Inspector. All I could make out was that it was a woman. I don't know how I know it but I know. Perhaps it was the shape of the hair.'

'That won't help you an awful lot, Inspector,' said Luke. 'Those houses were built to attract the first-time buyer and they're small. Single people buy them and also young couples. The couples usually move down into the town when the family starts to arrive. When the chicks leave the nest their parents may come back as a couple but there's also a high percentage of widows.'

'Like me,' said Helena.

'I don't think that there are many like you,' Luke said. Helena gave him a glowing look.

Ian Fellowes cleared his throat to call the meeting to order. 'What you're saying is that there's a high percentage of ladies, many of them single. According to the ambulance staff, you may have saved her life. Her injuries were recent but she was close to death. That suggests that the person you saw driving away may have been leaving the scene, either of an accident or of a deliberate assault with a motor vehicle.'

For several minutes the inspector asked Helena about the vehicle and driver. He questioned her gently, coming back to each aspect from another direction, but she could add nothing further. They agreed that the driver of the other vehicle might have been a small man with long hair.

'This is all very well,' Luke said at last. 'We understand your concern. But we might understand it better if you told us a little. The hospital staff refused to speculate. What were her injuries? Was she run over?'

Inspector Fellowes regarded him seriously for some seconds. Then, evidently deciding that Luke was entitled to the information and would soon receive it from the doctors anyway he said, 'She was crushed against the wall, apparently by a vehicle reversing against her.'

'So it could have been an accident and a panicked driving-away?'

'That's possible. Unlikely but possible. There are certain dark tyre-marks that could be a sign of sudden braking or of a driver accelerating away. Our Traffic officers were uncertain.'

'I would have thought that you could do more towards identifying the vehicle from the injuries. Height of the bumper and that sort of thing.'

'In theory you're right, Mr Grant,' said the inspector. He sighed. 'Unfortunately we can't. She was carrying a large carton of groceries, which took the impact and transferred it to her body. She seems to have bought the groceries earlier in the supermarket in the Square. The circumstances present us with a problem. On the basis of a preliminary report, my superiors in Edinburgh insist on considering it a traffic accident. But my colleagues locally in Traffic are positive that it must have been a deliberate act. So for the moment it ends up as my responsibility but I don't get any extra resources.'

'That's tough,' Luke said.

'Well yes, it is.'

Helena began a sympathetic gesture and opened her mouth. Luke thought that she was about to say, 'There there,' but she must have reconsidered in time. Instead she said, 'If there's anything we can do...'

'Well,' said Inspector Fellowes. He coughed and said, 'Well,' again. He made up his mind to go on. 'I have no business and no right to ask for help from individual members of the public. But the ladies of Birchgrove have so far proved unhelpful. Friday evening seems to be a busy time around here. It was ladies' night in the fitness centre and there was a bridge tournament in the hotel. The ladies – and gentlemen – are quite prepared to say which event they attended but they get very vague when asked about times and plead complete amnesia when asked who else was there and at what times and who had ever quarrelled with Mrs Highsmith.'

'They all have their naughty little secrets,' Luke said, avoiding Helena's eye. 'Each is probably afraid of starting an avalanche of exposures.'

'Well, I suppose you'd...' The inspector broke off. 'Forget I spoke,' he said.

Luke was abashed to realize how far his reputation had spread. To say nothing would have made the silence worse. 'You were about to say you'd suppose I'd know,' he said. 'I've lived here for a long time, close to an area that abounds with single women, and I've been a widower for more than fifty years. It would be surprising if my name hadn't been linked with a few of the neighbouring ladies. Only in loose gossip, of course.'

'Of course,' said his listeners in unison.

The inspector cleared his throat. 'Each of you has an interest in the truth. I can't have you bustling about and doing my job for me,' he said. 'But if in the course of general chat you should happen to pick up any information as to who had quarrelled with Mrs Highsmith and who was where and at what times, and more importantly who can confirm that information, please bring it straight to me. And now I must go.'

Luke saw him out. Helena had followed them. 'You won't stay to lunch?' Luke asked her.

'Can't. I have a guest coming. I'll call you later.' The inspector's car was already around the first bend. She gave him a quick peck on the cheek.

The girls were in the garden, playing some game with Pepper and a ball. No doubt it would be hard on the grass but he supposed that that was a small price to pay for keeping all three of them occupied. He went inside and up the stairs. When he came down again he was frowning. He went into the kitchen and made himself a toasted cheese sandwich with a little chopped tomato for his lunch. As he supposed, the aroma soon brought the girls in through the back door.

'Do we not get any lunch?' Jane asked.

Luke hardened his heart. 'I don't cook for girls with untidy bedrooms,' he told them. 'When you've done your job, I'll do mine. Violet, you were in charge.'

Violet twined her legs together and looked five years younger. 'We did tidy our rooms,' she said. It was almost a whine. 'But then Pepper came upstairs and a game started and somehow they got untidy again. This isn't the same untidy.'

The judgement of Solomon was required if a clash of wills was to be avoided. 'In that case,' he said, 'I'll make you some lunch. That counts for the first tidying up. After lunch you can tidy again and then, just to see that the rooms stay tidy, you can mow the grass. That's your job from now on.'

Rather to his surprise, both the argument and the task were accepted. While he made them a snack and put fruit and cheese on the table to please young appetites, he considered the future. The house would need vacuum-cleaning and he could probably count on them to go on leaving their rooms in turmoil. It was, he thought, a shame to take the money.

Five

Helena returned in the early afternoon. They could have had the house to themselves. A smooth whirring sound from outdoors suggested that the girls were pleasantly occupied on the lawn. Luke had inspected their rooms and found that they came just within an acceptable standard of tidiness although he suspected that the inside of the drawers would not.

The fine weather was continuing and they wanted to make the most of it while it lasted, so Luke had carried out a pair of folding chairs and they sat in the partial shade of a chestnut tree, the dappled light stirring gently and lending Helena an aspect of youth. At around the time of World War One, Luke's father, who had been an insurance agent with a flourishing business, had allowed a building contractor to pay off a bad debt by laying a terrace of green Westmoreland stone paving outside the French windows and sheltering it with a low wall backed by a hedge of cotoneaster. They kept Pepper with them because dogs and lawn-mowers can make an unhealthy mix. They could see the girls at work, one pushing the mower while the other, if not required to control the electric cable, took a turn re-cumbent on the old sofa in the summer-house. As long as the sound of the mower continued there was little danger of their being overheard.

'I just phoned again,' Luke said. 'She's still holding her own. They hope to have her stable enough for surgery by tomorrow morning.'

'That's good,' Helena said without en-thusiasm. 'Isn't it?'

'I don't know. They couldn't make me any promises about what faculties she'd still have. Apparently her head took a whack in addition to all the crushing. But it's not all bad, except for her. At least I'm getting to know my great-granddaughters.'

They sat in contemplative silence. After several minutes, Luke shuddered and gave himself a little shake. He said, 'This is a pretty kettle of fish.'

'That's what I was thinking,' Helena said. 'Your granddaughter-in-law – is that right? – gets knocked down. The supercops in Edinburgh treat it as a traffic accident. Local traffic Bobbies think it was deliberate and want to hand it over to the local CID man. He in turn doesn't know what to think, hasn't the resources to deal with it and can't get any sense out of the local ladies, each of whom is probably scared that a word out of place would bring down the wrath of the others on her head and result in her own sins being dragged into the light of day.'

'That's about the size of it. You might not think that so many women would have sins to be sensitive about, but in such small communities the majority take their attitudes from the local leaders.'

Helena was nodding. She looked over the hedge but the girls were fully occupied. 'I've only been here a few years,' she said, 'but from the moment I arrived I could see that there was quite a lot of sleeping around and not all of it heterosexual. There are lesbians at the bottom of my garden. Widows seem to gravitate here, and they've been accustomed to sex on tap.'

Luke wanted to say that he knew it. He

had been one of the very few unattached men in the vicinity and somebody, quite possibly Ella Gilbert, had talked. From being a handsome and virile-looking young man he had progressed into becoming an older man with the look of an elder states-man but still with that faintly piratical air and an intriguing limp. He had kept his figure and most of his hair. He could afford to dine a lady well and to buy her gifts. He could also produce flattering portraits or even glamour shots, depending on the direction of her aspirations. He was one of the few men to be sole occupant of a house – and a house, moreover, that could be approached discreetly, unseen and without setting tongues wagging. His youthful vigour, which had been above average, had diminished only slowly over the many years of his active life, during which period his understanding of the needs of a woman had become encyclopaedic. He had also had a vasectomy, thus obviating the need for cer-tain embarrassing rituals. As a result he was usually marked at least nine out of ten whenever such topics came up in exclusively female company, as they are inclined to do. Luke had therefore received over the years more offers, direct or circumspect, than he could possibly have accepted.

But this was not a subject to be discussed with his current mistress. Luke said, 'What was happening locally on Friday night?'

'There was the bridge tournament in the Newton Lauder Hotel.'

'And a darts match in the Canal Bar. Not really a woman's scene but some may have gone with their partners.'

'And Friday night is ladies' night at the gym.'

'So it is!' said Luke. 'I'd forgotten that. Who's the biggest gossip in Birchgrove?' Helena looked blank. 'You've lived among them for the past few years,' he said. 'You must have noticed which of the ladies spreads the most tittle-tattle.'

'I don't mix very much,' Helena said. 'And you keep me pretty well occupied socially.'

'A couple of evenings a week at the most? Oh, come on!' he said. 'There's hardly a woman born who doesn't chat with neighbours. You must have been asked to one or two coffee mornings.'

'Well ... I suppose you could ask Angela McWilliam.'

At the mention of the name, Luke's memory again retreated into the past. Angela McWilliam had been the life and soul of many a party, always bubbling with jollity. Luke had known her to speak to without really coming to know her until they met by chance at a party in Edinburgh, hosted by a magazine for which she wrote fashion articles and he hoped to take the photographs. The venue was one of the better hotels.

Luke had previously rather steered clear of her. She was a forceful lady with a firm jaw and a firmer manner. It had been suggested that after sex she ate her partner although none of the male residents had turned out to be missing. After several drinks – and few drinks are more potent than free drinks – she was much less formidable. The ebb and flow of bodies had drifted them together and the banality of the other guests kept them there. They were surprised to find each other's conversation wittier than they had realized. Their talk and laughter became more personal. Suddenly she asked, 'Is it true that your right eye's artificial?'

'Quite true,' he said. 'But I can see with it. It's one of the wonders of modern technology.' Temptation rose up and ran away with him. Those were the days when it was quite likely to do so. With the ease of practice he slipped the glass eye out of its socket and, holding it in the palm of his hand, lowered it to a position below the hem of her skirt. 'Beautiful,' he said. 'Just beautiful. I never realized how lovely the unseen part of you is.'

Evidently Angela had heard and believed the gossip that circulated about him. 'To think,' she said, 'that all of it could be yours.'

Luke slipped out to the desk. Angela followed him. Upstairs in the expensive double room that he had had to engage for the whole night, he had occasion to repeat his remark. He survived the night and the following morning without more than a few and shallow tooth-marks.

This was the first of several such meetings. They went well together. But she was in need of a husband to provide for her other needs and he had made it clear that he was not going to marry again. Soon she became engaged to a magazine commissioning editor. Luke took the photographs at the wedding and gave the couple a crystal rose-bowl that had featured in a set of photographs that he took for an upmarket store.

Her husband, who had lived for his work, had not survived retirement. She had returned to Newton Lauder and was once again the life and soul of many a party. Luke had rather avoided her. He did not want any do-you-remembers in this company.

'I wouldn't know how to get in touch with her without being too obvious,' Luke said. 'If I start asking questions – and I haven't made up my mind yet – and if the fact becomes generally known, people may clam up.'

'That's in addition to the fact that you might be inviting another accident with another Land Rover,' Helena said.

'I won't stand against any walls and I'll be ready to jump. Anyway, how many years have I got to lose?' Luke asked rhetorically. 'I owe it to the memory of my grandson. Could you find out for me...?'

'No, I could not,' Helena said with force.

'You're afraid that it's your turn to be run over?'

'I'm afraid of being sued.'

'I'd forgotten that you used to work as a legal secretary. But I don't think that there's anything libellous in finding out where somebody was on a particular evening.'

'Perhaps not,' she said. 'But there's also the question of who she had had a quarrel with. That's absolutely loaded with legal shrapnel.'

'And you haven't heard of any particular spats?'

'My dear, dozens of them. Not many of them serious enough to bring about a murderous assault. But you never know. Your granddaughter-in-law has a vitriolic tongue and these things can fester. Read the reports of trials and you'll be amazed at how many murderous assaults have taken place for reasons that you or I would consider insignificant.'

The sound of the mower had stopped again. They craned their necks but Jane was emptying the hopper of the mower onto the compost heap and mixing the cuttings with torn newspapers. Violet seemed to be asleep on the couch in the summerhouse. 'Who runs the bridge club tournaments?' Luke asked.

'The minister's wife, usually. When she's away, which I think she is just now, Molly Calder takes it on.'

Luke sighed in relief and expressed silent thanks for one lady with whom he had not had a relationship. He could speak to Molly Calder with no do-you remembers. He would not have wished to approach the minister's wife – not because of any past affair between them but because she had let him know, by subtle language of the face and body and most especially her prominent nose, that she considered him to be an instrument of the devil.

When the mower started up again, he craned his neck to see over the hedge. Jane was still pushing while Violet seemed to have awoken and was manipulating the cable. He waved to catch Violet's eye and beckoned. She joined them, fetching out another folding chair.

'This isn't for Jane's ears yet,' Luke said. (Violet's eyes widened. Young girls love a secret.) 'The police aren't sure that the accident to your mother was altogether accidental. They want to make sure, one way or the other. They'd like to know who your mother quarrelled with.'

Violet sat silently for a minute, digesting the import of the words. She did not appear wholly surprised or even shocked. Then she said slowly, 'Mum has a sharp tongue. She can snap at people. She doesn't always mean it but she takes offence very easily and when her back's up she can sort of lash out. You know what I mean? And she has a way with words that can hurt.'

'And then she's both hurt and surprised when people take offence at what she says?' Luke suggested.

'Yes. How did you know? Had she given you the sharp edge of her tongue?'

'Often, but that's not how I knew. I know the type. Go on.'

'I think,' Violet said as though solving an eternal puzzle, 'that that's why she doesn't have any close friends. She forgets straight away whatever she said but they don't and it goes on rankling.'

'Do you remember anybody in particular?'

'Only this much.' Violet paused for thought again. 'Marigold Hick and Mrs Benton. I remember one or two other quarrels and I remember her saying that somebody shouldn't have said whatever it was. But those are only the ones I know about because I was there or because she moaned about it to me which she didn't usually do. She seemed to be in a cold and formal way of speaking to almost everybody. You know what I mean?'

'I know exactly what you mean,' Luke said. 'Think about it and jot down what you remember, ready to tell me. And this is not for talking about, remember?'

'I'll remember.'

'The other thing is that it would be helpful to know who was out and about on Friday evening; who was at the bridge tournament and so on. You can't go around asking a whole lot of questions but you could listen.'

Violet nodded wisely. 'I could. And I know one person I could ask. Roddy McWilliam. He's my friend.' Violet turned pink. 'He's a year or two older then me.'

Luke glanced at Helena but she was watching a thrush in the upper branches of the chestnut tree. 'Is his mother named Angela?' he asked.

'I think so. Yes, I'm sure she is. And she seems to be into everything. Would it be all right if I asked him, in confidence? I could make him promise.'

'But would he keep his promise?'

'Oh, I think so,' she said airily. Luke thought that she was beginning to know but not to understand her power as an attractive female. 'He keeps wanting to kiss me,' she explained. 'Why do boys do that?'

Luke was aware of both pleasure and dismay ... pleasure that she had retained her innocence past the age at which most would have been educated by their mothers or their classmates, pleasure also that she had asked the question of him, but dismay that it might become his duty to furnish that information. It said much about the strictness of their upbringing.

'Do your friends at school not talk about it?'

'Sometimes. But that's only bits and pieces that don't connect up and you're never sure if they're joking. And if you ask questions you're only showing your ignorance.'

'I see. Well, one of these days your hormones will tell you why boys want to kiss you. I'm not going to tell you bits of the subject, that would be a sure way to add to your confusion, but next time that we have an hour or two spare together and Jane isn't listening, we'll sit down and I'll tell you all about it. In the meantime, don't do him favours of that sort. Did your mother never explain to you?'

'I didn't dare to discuss it with her. She'd

only have said that I wasn't ever to see him again, which would've been a bit difficult as we go to the same school.'

Luke decided that it was high time that boundaries were drawn. He considered passing the task over to Helena but she was looking both amused and distant. He continued, watching Helena's face for warnings that he was going wrong. 'Holding hands is all right,' he said, 'but that's as close as his hands go. A friendly hug is OK but it must be quick and then separate.'

Violet was listening, big-eyed, and digesting every word. 'What about this kissing business?' she asked.

'You're only sixteen,' he said.

'Nearly seventeen.'

'Even so, what do your friends at school do?'

'Huh! They talk a lot of talk but I don't believe the half of it. I can tell by the way they talk and look at each other that they don't even believe each other.'

'You're probably right. If he pecks you on the cheek that's acceptable, provided that you don't mind.' Luke paused to gather his wits. He was trying to walk a line between permissiveness and the fuddy-duddy and recalling that his own genes were in there somewhere. 'A kiss on the lips is permissible at the end of an evening. But definitely no tongues. Not at your age. If he pushes his tongue into your mouth bite it.'

'Off?' Violet squeaked. She did not seem to be as shocked as he would have liked.

Luke became conscious of a great dichotomy. Part of him remembered a time when he had believed with fervour that the world would be a better place if the girls were freer with their favours. But these were now *his* girls, carriers of his genes, and he did not want his genes contaminated. He fought off the temptation to give an affirmative answer. 'No, not right off. Just a hard enough nip that he won't do it again in a hurry. When we have our talk I'll explain about the limits ... and the dangers.'

Jane's head appeared suddenly over the hedge. 'I've done all I'm going to do,' she said.

Violet sighed and got up. 'I suppose I'd better go and clear up the mess,' she said.

'Welcome to the club,' said Luke. 'Can you stay to dinner?' he asked Helena. 'I asked the butcher for sliced roast beef for four but I think he's given me enough for ten.'

'I can't. Don't worry about it. Two teen-agers will soon eat it down to size.'

Luke returned to his workroom and made a serious attempt to catch up with overdue work.

Six

Luke had at least a nodding acquaintance with Molly Calder through her husband, Keith. Keith Calder was the proprietor of the sports shop in Newton Lauder; primarily a shop dealing in guns and fishing tackle but carrying also a stock of material allied to other sports. Here might come the skateboard addict, the racing cyclist or the hangglider enthusiast; if the shop did not have whatever the client wanted, it would be obtained for him and, if desired, an expert would be found to give advanced instruction.

Luke had kept up his contact with Keith by purchasing regular supplies of fishing tackle at the shop. But their acquaintance ran deeper than that. Keith had been a schoolboy during Luke's courtship and marriage. There had followed a period during which they might have seemed to be competing for the title of local stud. This could have turned them into bitter enemies, but in fact although their paths might have crossed they had never collided. Keith had eventually married Molly and mended his ways with only occasional lapses; and he had watched with nostalgia what some considered to be the resumed rake's progress of Luke. Keith was supremely happy with Molly and his daughter. He would not willingly have lost them nor hurt Molly by being noticeably unfaithful, but there were times when Luke, who, in consoling himself for the death of Hannah, had put behind him the constraints of marriage, seemed to have it made.

There was one extra reason for Luke to consult Molly. Keith's expertise in ballistics had resulted in his often being consulted, by the police or the defence, in cases where firearms were involved. This had led to his often becoming involved in other matters of crime. His natural curiosity, allied to a sense of justice, had gained him a reputation and, although he always resented being called a private eye, that was in effect what he had often become. He might prove to be a valuable source of advice.

Luke picked up the phone and keyed the number. A cheerful and not unmusical voice answered.

'Mrs Calder?'

'Yes.'

'It's Luke Grant. You may remember...?'

'I remember you very well, Mr Grant.'

'I'm hoping that you can help me. I believe you were running the bridge tournament on Friday evening and I was looking for some information about who was present.'

'Oh? Perhaps you should tell me why you need this?' Molly answered.

'Of course. It's for Inspector Fellowes. He's looking into my granddaughter's accident and is hoping to find a witness or two.'

'Well, I'd be happy to help. I was sorry to hear about the accident. Anyway, yes, I have a list,' she said. 'There's nothing confidential about it. I can run a copy off on the computer. Shall I email it to you?'

Luke thought that there might be some questions to ask and he wanted to see her face when he asked them. 'I'm not very clever about e-mails,' he said, 'and I've just changed my service provider. Could I come and collect it?'

'We're going out shortly,' she said, 'but we're planning to take a bar meal in the Newton Lauder Hotel. Would you like to meet me there? The small cocktail bar at the back...'

'That would be fine.'

The thought of preparing a Sunday evening meal for three had been beginning to loom and he had forgotten to take the sliced roast beef out of the freezer. He called the girls. They came in from the garden, dusted with grass clippings and other garden debris. He fetched a clothes-brush. 'Dust yourselves down with this before you come in. Then go and shower and change into something smart. We're going to dine out.'

Violet set about brushing Jane. 'We'll have to go past Cayley. We only have country togs here.'

'There won't be hot water there. Hop in the Land Rover and we'll collect what we need and come back here.'

He had the keys to Cayley in his pocket. He took the girls to the front door. While they gathered up some more respectable garb he walked to the garage court. It was only one house away and on the same side of the street. The path led him in through the narrow slot between the end garage and the screen wall and continued out through a matching slot on the further side. Here was where Emily had been so badly injured. Dried blood would not show on the brick but there were stains on the mortar joints and when he stood back with half-closed eye he could see a vague shape in human scale. Standing with his back to it, he was looking along a narrow road between two rows, each of about ten lock-up garages. He could imagine Emily coming from her own lock-up, which as he recalled it was near the middle of the row to his left. She would have been carrying her carton of groceries and heading for the path to his right. If a vehicle had backed or driven suddenly out of one of the garages and come towards her, she would probably have stood just about where he was, waiting for it to be driven away.

But to drive away, the driver would have had to reverse the length of the garage court if he was not already facing that way. A sort of pattern began to gel. The road between the garages was not very generous – most of the metal doors showed dents and scrapes where a driver had misjudged his or her turn. To collide with a pedestrian standing where he was, in forward gear or reverse, the vehicle would have to be hauled round hard. He tried to imagine it but had difficulty visualizing it as an accident. It was not a manoeuvre to be carried out at speed.

The tarmac roadway between the lock-ups had been driven over for years but not usually in a hurry. Standing where Emily had stood, he could see the faint skid-marks referred to by DI Fellowes. They ended almost at his feet. But had they been a desperate attempt to brake before hitting a pedestrian or a violent use of the clutch and throttle as a guilty person fled the scene? If the police, with their facilities and expertise, had been unable to make the distinction, he would have even less chance.

He retraced his path towards Cayley. A man of about forty had emerged from Cayley between that house and the garages. If anyone had heard the sounds of vehicles, this would be the man. 'Excuse me,' Luke said.

The man raised one finger to his ear in the typical gesture of one who is turning on a hearing aid. 'I beg your pardon?' he said.

Suffice to say that this neighbour had heard nothing that night.

The girls had filled another cardboard box. Luke was sure that they had brought all sorts of contraband but he had missed his afternoon nap and was becoming too tired to argue. He snatched a few minutes of rest while the girls showered and then he roused and made himself respectable. He had not been in the habit of troubling too much with his appearance. Clients did not expect it of a photographer but he would prefer that his great-granddaughters saw him in a different light. He changed into pale slacks and a blazer with a club tie, made use of his electric shaver and brushed his hair. As an afterthought, he trimmed his eyebrows. The mirror showed him a younger and more respectable version of himself.

When they forgathered in the hall he was very much taken with the girls' appearance. For years he had seen them only occasionally, and Emily had never encouraged them to impress him. Now, washed and changed into light summer frocks (slightly in need of a press) they made a charming picture. Their hair was the chestnut brown of their mother's but brushed and brushed until it had taken on a gloss that enhanced the natural waves. Jane had all the grace of the young girl, still slightly immature in a snub-nosed and bony way, but Violet, now nearly a woman but a very young one, had the advantages of both youth and maturity. She was still long-legged and coltish but with the beginning of a womanly bosom and hips. She would soon have the boys slavering and he hoped that their mother would be back on her feet before he had to do much about it. The duties of the chaperon were not where his talents lay. He made up his mind that there would be a shoe-cleaning morning very shortly.

'You look nice,' Violet told Luke.

'You both do me great credit,' he told them. 'See that your manners live up to that. We're all much too smart for this tatty old Land Rover,' he added as they neared the B-road.

'We could have washed it for you,' Jane said. 'That might have helped.' She was sitting sidesaddle in the centre seat.

'It would have stayed clean for about five minutes, the way the roads are around here,' said Violet. 'And at least it won't matter if you put another dent in it.'

Luke was a little hurt. The Land Rover

had been his personal transport, almost his friend, for a long time. 'Not an awful lot,' he agreed. He took a quick look but their seat belts were fastened.

'GG,' Violet said, 'I think I want a bra. Mum said I was too young but I'm beginning to feel the need. What do you think?'

'We'll ask Mrs Highsmith,' Luke said. 'But I think you're probably right.'

'GG, you're not looking.'

'I have to watch the road.'

'You could at least look at her,' Jane said. Luke could detect very faintly a shared giggle.

Luke drew aside into a bus lay-by. The likelihood of a bus at that time of a Sunday evening was very remote. 'Any time that you feel like setting out to embarrass me,' Luke said, 'go right ahead; but just remember that I can give as good as I get. I may just ask you in public if you have clean knickers on.'

'You're beautiful when you're angry,' Violet said.

'Where on earth did you pick up that expression?' he asked. Had somebody ever said it to her?

Violet was blushing scarlet. 'I heard somebody say it in a film on the box and I saved it up. I've been waiting for a chance to use it.'

'Well, don't use it again.' He drove on.

In the Newton Lauder Hotel, tucked away behind the lounge and between the public bar and the dining room there is a small cocktail bar patronized only by discerning locals. It is presided over by a plump but friendly and not unbeautiful lady. Bar meals may be obtained there thanks to a convenient hatch to the kitchens. Those familiar enough to use it also know to guard their tongues, because the lady happens to be the wife of the premier local solicitor and secrets whispered over a dram or a glass of the house red have been known to surface in court.

The bar, when they arrived, was uninhabited except for a man reading the paper in a corner and the lady behind the bar. They took occupation of another corner where two tables, each of which was too small for a party of five, could be and often were pushed together, in a position convenient to the hatch.

The two girls put their heads together over the menu while their great-grandfather went to the bar for a pint of Bass, a small shandy and a breakfast orange. It was Luke's experience that he only had to be standing at a bar with money in his hand for everybody that he knew to arrive. Courtesy would then oblige him to offer the first comers a drink and before that transaction was completed another party of his dearest friends would appear. Not that he was mean, but his income had reduced considerably as he aged while the cost of living seemed to have shot through the roof; and he now seemed to have taken on two more wide open mouths, like hatchlings, to feed. But these hatchlings had bodies to clothe and did not grow their own feathers. How long this drain on his resources would last only time would tell.

Just as he feared, the motherly barmaid had heard of the accident to Emily and identified him as Emily's grandfather-in-law. The identities of the girls followed on. The process of making change was considerably slowed by the need to enquire after Emily's progress (about which Luke was still unable to give a categorical answer) and how the girls were settling down with their elderly progenitor. Thus, at the very moment when she was about to hand Luke his change, Keith and Molly Calder walked in. Like Luke, they had worn well. Molly had always been inclined to plumpness but she had managed to keep it in check and only her worst enemy would have called her fat. Keith had kept most of his hair although it was now mostly grey; and there was still an athletic spring in his step. They accepted a double malt whisky and a large glass of the house red. Luke reminded himself that he had saved all his life for his old age and this was it.

As planned, they pushed two tables together. They ordered. The barmaid passed their orders through the hatch and lingered for a moment to chat, but soon they had comparative privacy. The hatch was firmly closed.

Molly produced an envelope. Keith engaged the girls in small talk and soon there were whispers and giggles at that end of the table – by prior arrangement, Luke was sure.

'Here's that list for Inspector Fellowes.' Molly beamed, showing a very pretty set of teeth, as she handed the envelope over. 'We're acquainted. He married our daughter.'

'There's a conversation-stopper if ever

there was one. I wonder why he didn't ask you himself.'

'He's rather hard-pressed just now,' Molly said. 'It suits the bosses in Edinburgh to believe that things like your granddaughter's – granddaughter-in-law's is it? – injuries were accidental until proved otherwise. They're very short-staffed and overloaded since the cuts, so they don't want to send scarce and valuable resources into the backwoods, looking for foul play where they don't think that it exists. Ian doesn't believe that it was a hit and run, so he's spreading himself and his very few men very thin.'

'Is he really asking for my help? Or is he being devious and hoping that we'll incriminate ourselves over something?'

Molly laughed. 'He isn't as devious as that! Only to the extent of deviously persuading the public to help him out. It's surprising how well it sometimes works out for him.'

Luke accepted the envelope and weighed it in his hand. 'This is everybody who played in the bridge tournament? Were they all there until the bitter end?'

'I'm fairly sure of it. It was a needle match to the end and then there were prizes to give out. We didn't finish until midnight and even after that some of the players wanted to linger and hash over the evening's play. We almost had to drive them out so that the janitor could lock up the hall.'

'That's very helpful,' Luke said thoughtfully. While they spoke, his next few steps began to materialize out of the mist. 'So your son-in-law can forget about anybody on this list. The other event that seems to have attracted some of the locals was the darts match in the Canal Bar.'

'I can help you again,' Molly said. 'My brother Ronnie captains the local darts team. Have you met him? He's large and rugged. Rough-hewn describes him.'

Luke smiled wryly. 'It describes quite a few of the local men.'

'So it does. Never mind. I'll ask him what time it finished and to make a list of anyone who stayed after that.'

'You're being so helpful that I may as well ask you about ladies' night at the gym.'

'That's an easy one,' Molly said, laughing. 'Friday's the night when all the man things happen, so it's ladies' night at the gym. But most of the ladies have other things to do on a Friday, so Tuesday's their night. On Fridays only Meg Brionie goes to the gym because she's getting special training for the Scottish Netball Team.'

'That's all, then?'

'I think so.'

Their meal was served just then. Conversation at the other end of the table became disjointed. Luke felt that he had to drop the subject, which was anyway doomed. Jane had been observing what she saw on the ground, the release pens, feeders, watering points, shelters, sunning rides and cage traps for magpies; and she had a dozen questions about each of them. Those subjects were close to the hearts of the adults present and soon there was hot debate as to why sparrowhawks were protected when they were so common. Two gamekeepers who had come into the bar joined in and got quite heated on the subject.

Seven

Keith had insisted on an exchange of rounds. After the unaccustomed volume of beer, Luke had had to rouse several times during the night. Not surprisingly, then, the two girls, who had slept as only the young can do, were once again up and about before him. They had breakfasted and fed Pepper and it was only the sound of their playing pig-in-the-middle with the dog on the lawn that woke him. An untidy kitchen and an awakening when he might have slept a little longer were a small price to pay for their compliant spirit. They would sometimes test the boundaries of his tolerance, he realized, but in the main they were surprisingly well behaved without seeming in any way repressed. Or was this, he wondered, only because they were secretive in their naughtiness and clever with it. No, he decided, definitely they were good girls. He decided that he would be rather sorry when the time came to return them to their mother.

Sunday shopping had been late coming to Newton Lauder but he had managed some necessary purchases. He had rather splashed out in treating himself to several pairs of pyjamas and a fancy dressing gown, but he had no immediate excuse to show them off. He readied himself for the day, swallowed a quick breakfast and made a phone call. As he set off with his new if temporary family for the now customary dogging-in walk he said, 'I phoned the New Royal. Your mother came through another night a little stronger. She's going into surgery now. They said not to come in, we couldn't see her and she wouldn't know us anyway; and there's no point sending in anything edible because she'll be fed through tubes for some time to come. She may be able to appreciate flowers tomorrow so we'll think about sending a bouquet by Interflora.'

That information seemed to make the great change to their lives more real, so that they were dumbstruck for the moment. Then Jane said, 'She doesn't hurt, does she?' in a strangled voice.

'No. They're keeping her asleep. And when they let her wake up, after the operation, they'll keep her dopey until she's ready to feel better.'

Jane breathed again. 'That's not so bad then.'

There was another silence. Jane sent Pepper to push the birds out of a jungle of gorse. She was developing a talent for dog-work, which helped to keep her mind off her mother. Violet had the same knack but in Jane he could see the dawning of fascination.

Out of the blue, Violet said, 'Roddy wants me to go to Craggan Water with him this afternoon. He's going to teach me trout-fishing. Is it all right if I go?'

Luke glanced up at the sky while he suffered a rush of conflicting thoughts. The day was bright and calm but rather cool, far from ideal for trout fishing. This might be the beginning of teenage boy problems, but with luck they would be left for her mother to resolve. On the up side, at least she had asked him. He could use this one stone to kill a whole flock of birds. Craggan Water was too shallow to drown in.

'That will be all right,' he said, 'provided

that you take Jane with you.'

'Oh, GG!'

'What did you want to do that she should not witness?' Violet didn't answer except by turning slightly pink. He went on. 'I have a lot to do and I'll be relieved if she's being looked after.'

'I don't need looking after,' Jane protested.

'Yes, you do,' said Violet.

'I *don't*.'

'You do too,' said Luke. 'But if you do this for me, and promise to be both good and careful, I'll lend Violet my trout rod and Jane my little brook rod. You can both practise casting on the lawn before lunch and then you won't show yourselves up. In fact, you'll be able to amaze Roddy with the speed at which you learn. How about that?'

Jane nodded uncertainly. Violet said 'I suppose so.'

'Good. While you're about it you could, without making it seem important, sound Roderick out as to whether he knows about any particular quarrels your mother had with any of the other ladies round about. Or men, come to that.'

Violet made a small sound of concurrence. They walked on to the end of that field. Pepper disappeared into the weeds lining a ditch. Jane climbed a gate and went to see what was delaying her.

'By the way, Jane knows that somebody did that to Mum on purpose,' Violet announced quietly.

This particular nettle had to be grasped at some time. 'We don't know,' Luke said, struggling with a rusty bolt. 'I told you that before. It was almost certainly an accident but it does seem to be an unlikely one, and it was against the law for whoever did it to drive off, so it has to be looked into by the police. It's best not to talk about it to Jane.'

'She knows, though, that's why she's so quiet.'

'This is quiet?'

'For her, it's deathly silence.'

'Still, don't go on about it. We don't know for sure.' Luke paused in the act of re-bolting the gate and considered. 'Unless she asks something. Then use your discretion. If in doubt, refer her to me.'

'I understand.'

Jane came back with a soaking wet but happy Pepper at heel.

After an intensive casting lesson and an

early snack lunch, he saw them off in the care of Roddy McWilliam. Roddy appeared to be a well-behaved youth, perhaps romantic rather than lecherous; but that might have been said of himself in his youth. Luke had had a hunt through his fishing bag and had been able to furnish each of them with a reel and a line of suitable weight. Violet was carrying a net and his fly-box while Jane was swinging a priest in a manner suggesting that she was looking forward to stunning something about the size of a medium sized shark. Luke had scarcely seen Roddy in recent years but he had grown into a sensible-looking young man just a year or two older than Violet. He was also becoming a rather good-looking young man if you managed to ignore the protruding red ears. Luke could see breakers ahead but he hoped that they were a long way off.

When the fishing party had marched off towards Craggan Water, he phoned Helena. 'You missed a good meal last night,' he told her. 'We met the Calders.'

'I had a visitor coming. She does some sewing for me. I need her services. I'm dangerous with a needle.'

'I know. You told me – about the sewing, I

mean. Are you free? I want to pick your brains about the denizens of Birchgrove.'

'Don't count on me this afternoon.'

'That's too bad. Would you at least write me out a list of the occupants, with house numbers?'

'I don't know everybody,' she said hesitantly. 'I haven't lived here so very long.'

'Never mind,' he said. 'I can get it off the Internet.'

Luke spent the afternoon in his workroom. He finished sorting and editing shots for two clients and emailed off the chosen pictures. He copied what he wanted to keep on to recordable CDs and cleared the memories from his computer and the camera. Then he had time to find the rating roll on the Internet and print off the names and addresses of the Birchgrove denizens on to sheets of paper that he taped together and pinned to a wall. He put a pencil line through the name of anybody who he knew to be very young or old and then, uncertainly and in pencil, through the name of anybody masculine. This last was on the grounds that, firstly, Helena had thought that she had seen a woman driving away

116

from the accident scene and, secondly, that a woman was much more likely to quarrel terminally with another woman than with a man.

He had heard noises at his front door and had assumed that one or both girls had returned early. When he had not been interrupted he had returned his attention to his work. But when at last he straightened his back, yawned and got up, it was to find a large envelope just inside the front door.

There was a note from Molly Calder in a neat, round hand:

Dear Mr Grant,

I have seen my brother. I got him to write down a list of the people who played darts, in fact everybody that he could remember seeing in the Canal Bar on Saturday night. They had a late licence and I had him put an X against anybody who he was reasonably sure was still there when they closed up.

After trying to be helpful I may as well continue. Mrs Ilwand at Hay Lodge was having a dinner party that night. In fact, we were supposed to go but I was responsible for the bridge tournament and

Keith said that he wouldn't go without me. I'll find out who was there and let you know.

Yours sincerely,

Molly Calder (Mrs).

After putting a pencil line and a query through those who Ronnie was 'reasonably sure' had been in the Canal Bar until closing time, Luke still had eleven households whose occupants were at home, visiting each other or otherwise engaged. Assuming, of course, that the guilty driver was local; but the presence of the vehicle in the garage court made that a logical assumption. All the garages had regular users but a stranger was unlikely to have access to one of them. An unfamiliar Land Rover lurking in the access way could hardly be missed. One Land Rover may look very like another but a local resident finding a vehicle lurking in the access way of the garage court could be expected to glance inside and see who was in the driver's seat.

He found Angela McWilliam's number in an old personal phone book. But then he remembered that she had moved away and come back. Her new number was in the BT directory and he found it after a lengthy search. He updated his own book and then keyed the number.

'Hello. Angela McWilliam?'

'Yes.'

'This is a voice out of your past,' he said.

'Luke Grant,' she said. There was still a hint of the old mirth in her voice.

He carried the cordless phone over to the armchair in the corner of his workroom. It was half collapsing but it was comfortable. This was not going to be as quick a call as he had hoped. 'You couldn't possibly recognize my voice after all these years.'

Her laugh came back at full strength. 'Once heard never forgotten. But I was expecting you to call.' Her voice sobered. 'We all heard what happened to Emily Highsmith. Your what? Granddaughter?'

'In law.'

'Yes. And then her daughters are staying with you. My son seems to be getting soppy over one of them. And you were seen collecting luggage from her house. How is she?'

'Holding her own. I believe that they're operating just now. I may know more tonight.'

'We'll have to have a whip-round for

flowers. Anyway, you were taking a look at where it happened and then I bumped into Helena Harper in the Paki corner shop and she said that you might be looking me up, though what I could possibly tell you I really don't know.'

In Luke's recollection, Angela had always been able to take a ribbing in good part. He was tempted to say that, according to Helena, she was as big a chatterbox as ever. But if she took offence she might refuse to speak and might also spread the word around that he was asking more questions than was justified by a hit and run accident to a not very close relative. 'I'm told,' he said carefully, 'that you're still at the heart of local social life and that you hear everything that's going on. May I ask you something in absolute confidence?'

'Yes, of course.'

How much that assurance was worth Luke would have to guess. 'The suggestion has been made that what happened to Emily may not have been altogether accidental, unless it was the kind of accident driven by somebody's subconscious. It has been said that there's no such thing as an accident but I don't wholly go along with that.'

'I hope you're not getting the idea that I was driving the car that knocked her down!' Angela's voice conveyed genuine shock.

'Certainly not. You were at the bridge tournament. And, anyway, I haven't heard that you had a quarrel with her.'

There was silence on the line for several seconds. When Angela spoke again it was in subdued tones quite devoid of her usual gaiety. 'That's all you know. Somebody will probably tell you, and anyway I seem to have a shatterproof alibi, so I may as well spill the beans. I mean, the occasion was private but there's always somebody who overhears. That's if she didn't tell somebody herself but, if she did, it was probably a twisted version because she's that sort of person.'

'Do you know, I haven't the faintest idea what you're talking about?' Luke said.

'I'm coming to it. This happened two or three weeks ago at one of those informal gatherings that happen sometimes. I'd been down at the shops and I bumped into Janice Carter. She suggested that we have a sherry in the Hotel across the Square but I said that I wasn't dressed for that. If you're going into that place, you get the tiara out of pawn. We agreed to stop off at the Canal Bar. That's one place you can go straight from the garden or dressed in sackcloth and nobody gives a damn. A real spit-and-sawdust, but you probably know it better than I do.

'We met some of the neighbours in the Canal Bar and a party developed. Your granddaughter-in-law was there with some bloke. I remember I was telling some mildly blue but genuinely funny stories. The men were laughing their heads off and I think she may have been jealous. When I went to the little girls' room she followed me. Her back garden's back-to-back with mine and she accused me of tossing slugs and snails over the hedge when I was gardening. Absolute rubbish, of course, and I said so. Then she glanced into the cubicles to make sure that nobody was in there and she said something so unspeakably horrible that it took my breath away, which was probably her intention. She buggered off quickly before I could give her the slap that I was just working up to. And I'm definitely not going to tell you what she said because it was just too bad to repeat.'

Her voice had been rising and Luke had a

feeling that a cooling off period was required. He was sorely tempted to pursue the
topic of exactly what Emily had said to get
so very far up Angela's nose, but he decided
that that particular topic had better be left
to a more suitable occasion. 'I'll leave you to
think about it,' he said. 'Please jot down the
details of any quarrels you can remember
between Emily and any of her neighbours
and let me know later.'

'I'll do that. But why? I mean, if you wait
until you speak to her she can tell you who
ran her down.'

'She may not come out of the anaesthetic.'
He paused but there was no audible
reaction. He should have tried that gambit
face to face. 'People don't always. And anybody who's had a serious knock on the head
is liable to remember everything that happened except for what came immediately
before the injury. Her memory may return
later, but if we leave it that long other
peoples' memories will have faded.'

'I suppose that's true,' she said slowly.
Luke thought that she was recognising a
heaven-sent chance to begin a new round of
chatter. 'All right. I'll see what I can do.'

Luke was on the point of terminating the

call when one of her passing mentions came to the surface of his attention. 'Who was the man that she was with in the Canal Bar?' he asked.

'I haven't the faintest. I never saw him before or since. A sturdy looking man with some facial hair, I think. He didn't seem pleased to be seen in her company so he's probably married. Just one of those dates that pass in the night – or for a night, I suppose.'

Luke caught up with the household chores while mentally digesting the problems surrounding the accident to Emily Highsmith. The girls returned. It had fallen to Jane to catch the only fish of the day, a brown trout of several ounces, just large enough to be cooked and eaten but enough to kindle a passion for the pursuit. Luke suspected that an addict had been born. He discarded the hopeless tangles of fine nylon, retaining only the flies, gave the girls another few minutes of expert instruction in the fine art of casting and set them to practising on the lawn. Each had a twist of wool at the tip of the leader instead of a hook.

After the evening meal the girls went back

to their casting practice. Luke decided to phone the 'New Royal'. Emily, he learned, was still in intensive care but he was connected to the ward.

The ward sister was properly reluctant to discuss a patient. Luke said, 'Apart from two young daughters, I think I'm probably her next of kin. I'm quite sure that I'm her only other kin in Scotland.'

The ward sister relaxed. Evidently Luke's name also rang a bell. 'She came through surgery as well as could be expected,' he was told. 'There will be more operations to come. For the moment she's weak. She's sleeping again now, but for a while she came to. She was very muzzy but she's anxious to see Luke Grant.'

'That's who I am,' Luke said. 'When could I visit her?'

'Tomorrow. But leave it until after mid-morning. I'll try to arrange for her doctor to see you. Give me your phone number and I'll call you if there's any change.' With those ominous words Luke had to be content. He only told the girls that their mother had survived her surgery.

Luke phoned Helena. She took a long time

to answer the phone. 'I was in the garden,' she told him, 'trying to win it back from the Indians.'

'My great-granddaughters might be able to help you,' he told her. 'It looks as though I may be doing a lot of hospital visiting in the next few days – or weeks – and I was hoping that you might look after them now and again. They turn out to be amazingly well behaved and biddable, unless they're putting up a clever front, and they seem quite good in a garden. They enjoy having something positive to do.'

'I think that could be arranged.' He could hear the smile in her voice. 'They do seem to be good girls, which is quite a rarity these days.'

'Just don't stand any nonsense.'

'I won't. How's their mother doing?'

'She's had a lot of heavy surgery but there's more to come. She's in Intensive Care but the ward sister won't comment on her prospects, which is ominous. Usually they tell you brightly that there's no cause for concern. Meantime, Emily's asking for me and making it sound urgent. The girls want to see their mother and I think it might help them to see that she's still alive, but not while she's like a hedgehog with tubes and wires. I'll see how she looks tomorrow.'

In the morning, Luke phoned the 'New Royal' again. The same sister was back on duty. 'She's rousing from time to time,' she said, 'but then she keeps drifting off again. When she's awake she says that she wants to see you, very urgently, but quite rightly she says not to bring her daughters. What with bruising and bandages and connections to monitors, she's not a reassuring picture, definitely not for showing to young girls.'

'I can imagine,' Luke said.

'See for yourself. But leave it until this afternoon. She may be more alert by then.'

'Yes. Thank you. What are her chances?'

There was a brief but telling hesitation on the line. 'You'd have to ask the doctors about that.'

Helena was again slow to answer the phone. 'In the garden again?' he asked.

'Of course. At this time of year it's like painting the Forth Bridge. You get to the end of a flowerbed and look round and the weeds are coming up again behind you. It's all right for some. You have very little but grass and woodland.'

Luke smiled complacently. His parents, and later his wife, had been keen gardeners but when he became the sole occupant of the house and quite often away or abroad the burden of gardening had been too much for an ageing man with a damaged foot. Gradually he had replaced many of the commonplace trees, interspersing some fine old trees with flowering varieties and those with bright foliage. The flowerbeds had been grassed over. The result was a garden that usually looked attractive but needed little attention other than mowing; and if a protracted absence allowed the grass to get beyond the mower, he had a scythe. 'I can offer you helpers right away,' he said. 'I'm told that Emily wants to see me urgently. It may only be to resume the quarrel that we began last time we met or to tell me how the girls' hair should be washed, but I'd better go. The ward sister at the New Royal still won't even utter the usual platitudes, which I don't find reassuring, and both she and the patient are adamant that she isn't a sight for young eyes. I'll have my mobile on me, so if you have any problems you can call me.'

'I won't have any problems.'

★　★　★

It had long been Luke's opinion that the Edinburgh traffic system, after years of total neglect, was now in a carefully contrived struggle to make driving difficult and parking impossible. He had therefore been putting off a series of overdue errands and visits. If he left immediately he might manage to do several of them during the morning, have a late lunch with an old friend and still call on Emily during the afternoon. He checked that his mobile phone was fully charged before calling to the girls.

They were quite amenable to visiting Helena for the day, but declined his offer of a lift to her door, preferring to play an electronic game on his computer and then walk round to Helena's in plenty of time for lunch, taking Pepper with them. He filled a bag with the makings for their lunch and another with Pepper's dinner and made them promise to lock up with care. There was a very low risk of intruders in the area, but some of his equipment was worth real money.

His Land Rover was parked, as usual, at the gable of his house, facing into the farm track. It might be old and battered and

129

thirsty but at least, thanks to regular attention from Ledbetter Junior, it was reliable. It started, as usual, at the first touch of the switch. He took the farm road in low gear. He had a clear view at the junction and there was nothing coming so he pulled gently out into the B-road, changing up as gravity took over but staying in third.

When he touched the brake pedal for the first time he knew that something was very wrong. The pedal felt soft and the Land Rover was still picking up speed. He jerked up the handbrake but there was nothing there. With a sense of incredulity he found that he had become a passenger, unable to do much more than steer.

They were coming to the steepest part of the hill. He changed down into second and put the vehicle into four-wheel drive, but the momentary respite let the road speed build up. The engine was protesting shrilly. There were bends to come, with walls and trees, and he was sure that the car would roll if he tried to drag it round at such a speed. He tried to visualize the effect of declutching and dragging the gear lever into bottom gear, but if it would engage at all he was positive that it would tear the teeth off the gears or the guts out of the vehicle, leaving him without engine and therefore without its drag and without even power steering. He was on the tarmac, but the vehicle was being shaken and the engine noise had risen to a scream.

Exactly what he had feared happened. There was a rumble and clatter from somewhere beneath him, followed by a loud bang. The engine noise ceased. The Land Rover sounded happier but hurled itself forward down the hill. With the engine stopped he had, as he feared, lost the power-assistance to the steering. It was, he thought with the spare corner of his mind, like trying to steer an elephant by the tail. Straining his sinews he got round the first bend on shrilling tyres without quite overturning but he was sure that the vehicle had only been held upright by his willpower alone. The roadside was going by in a blur. The town was approaching at a terrifying speed. There was traffic facing him. He knew that if he allowed his mind to go blank, they would all die. One car slowed. Another pulled out to overtake and then pulled back in a hurry as he flashed past. The canal bridge was coming at him and he could tell that the Land

Rover would have had no chance of passing the double bend with the hump between even if the roof of a van had not been showing as it approached the bottleneck. Perception slowed.

He had one chance to survive and to let others live. Beyond a rough triangle of grass and gorse bushes the canal offered the only soft option. As the road bent to the left he managed to pull to the right. His wheels left the ground for a full second as he crossed the verge but still they remained upright. The wire fence parted with a twang and then trailed behind. The gorse bushes whipped at the car but at least they bled off some of his speed, which saved him from slamming into the further towpath. Instead, the bank fell away and he entered the water like a Labrador going after a retrieve. The spray, he was told later, made a spectacular rainbow. A woman and her baby in its pushchair on the towpath were soaked. The Land Rover nudged the far bank and then settled on the bed of the canal. The water only came to the bottom of the windows. For a few seconds something hissed and bubbled, then all was quiet. When the pressure equalized, he found that he could open his door quite easily. He floundered to the bank through muddy water and torn twigs of gorse. It was reminiscent of his rescue of Helena, but not so cold.

The woman with the pushchair was standing over him, obstructing his efforts to climb out. Her hair was hanging in rats' tails. Her baby was loudly expressing its discomfort but he could hear her voice. 'What did you want to go and do that for?' she demanded.

In the letdown after the adrenaline rush, Luke decided that a stupid question deserved a stupid answer. 'I wanted to see right up your skirt,' he said through gritted teeth.

The woman jumped back hastily and he had room to climb out on to the towpath against the drag of the water, dripping and squelching. A crowd was beginning to gather as people appeared, apparently out of nowhere.

Eight

At any time of calamity, watchers will appear out of an empty scene. Any stranded astronaut may expect to see little green spectators on a passing asteroid. Luke had steered the Land Rover for the emptiest scenery that he could see. Seconds later he seemed to have drawn a larger crowd than a football match. A less fraught look resolved this audience into a mere few dozen, but growing steadily. Half of these bystanders were content to stand and stare, filing away the event for future contemplation or discussion. The other half bombarded him and each other with questions and contradictory instructions. Luke found that a list of Things To Do was accumulating in his mind but without any idea as to which took priority. After trying his mobile phone and finding it dead – the second phone to be lost to him through aquatic disaster – he was just deciding to tell them all where to go and in what manner and then to start walking home for a change of clothes. Or to walk down to Ledbetter's garage for a hire car, a taxi or even to buy another Land Rover. Anything, if he could only get away from the rabble to somewhere quiet and order his thoughts.

Some relief arrived in the person of Audrey Shanks, nee Brownrigg. Her arrival was not usually so welcome. Their brief affair, some years earlier, had occurred due to a complete misunderstanding. He had decided to take lunch in a local café rather than cook yet again for one. A strapping, blonde lady, whose face was vaguely familiar, entered and sat down at his table, disturbing his enjoyment of a rather dry quiche Lorraine. 'You're a very naughty boy,' she said archly, 'making rude gestures.'

Evidently the incident she referred to had been recent. He admitted to himself that the making of rude gestures was not absolutely foreign to him. A quick mental process of elimination homed him in on the specific. He had been descending the hill that morning, in an even earlier Land Rover than the one now drowned in the canal, when a lady in an Audi arrived at a junction from his left. He had the right of way but there were cars behind each of them and he could see high probability of a logjam developing. It happened that he was holding a roll of peppermints in his left hand, which limited his movements. A flash of his headlamps seemed to have no meaning for her, so he beckoned her on, but he made the gesture palm up and with the middle finger of his hand, the other fingers being engaged with the peppermints. It seemed that she had mistaken the gesture for one of deep sexual significance and she was responding to it. At that time he had not been one to pass by such a bountiful supply of femininity. She expressed an interest in his house and he offered to show it to her.

She admired it room by room but she seemed to be expecting something more. When they reached his bedroom, he made a move to embrace her, but his overtures were greeted with only qualified enthusiasm until he realized that, as a naturally dominant woman, when it came to the boudoir she had a desire, not always fulfilled in this egalitarian age, to be dominated. Gathering his courage, because she looked at least as strong as he was, he seized her with force, imprisoning her arms. Her struggles appeared sincere but they would not have repelled a six-year-old.

Their romance had lasted for about a week before it became clear to him that it must not last much longer. For one thing, she was sexually voracious. Her occasional desire to be tied up was titillating, but at the time he had still been potent and he had neither wish nor need to continue down that road. Outside the bedroom, she was bossy. For another, she was just the sort of well-meaning do-gooder that he thought did more harm than the most determined anarchist or criminal. He had watched such people in action all his life. They never saw beyond the immediate effect of their activities to the later consequences. They would campaign for the suppression of whatever they considered undesirable, thus rendering it a must-have for the rest of the population. They would push the pendulum of public behaviour and political correctness so far that the return swing was both inevitable and extreme. They would fight for the human rights of the least worthy citizens and never mind the rights of the rest. In

137

government, they would ensure that an aggressor was compensated while thrift and self-defence were both penalised. Yet they were good people in their little ways and well intentioned, just inflicted with tunnel vision and very difficult to live with.

Luke had happened on an exchange of dialogue in Kipling – 'He means well,' 'Could you have damned him more completely?' That summed up his own feelings. On one occasion he was trapped into saying that he had hurried to volunteer to fight for his country in World War Two, but even if he were still of an age to fight he would not take up arms to defend what his country was fast becoming. The values that he had hurried to defend, at the cost of an eye and a limp, had been eroded to the point of invisibility. He might have been speaking in Mandarin but she did manage to extract enough meaning to realize that he was denigrating what she passionately desired. She chose to believe that he was only seeking an excuse to spank her into submission and he realized too late that she had offered him a perfect opportunity for a parting of the ways.

Desirable though she might be in body,

her attitudes were wholly contrary to his own. Her manner, too, was authoritarian. Sometimes she might concede victory in debate to the dominant male, making of it a gesture of unmistakable sexuality, but more often she would brook no opposition and would lay down the law with a bark. Luke sometimes thought that she would have made a good RSM for one of the better regiments.

For once the solution arrived almost before the problem had been identified. Luke was introduced to a man who was almost her male clone – a tall, toothy sandal-wearing vegetarian with legs hairy below his shorts but with a lascivious twist to his mouth. So Luke arranged a small lunch party at a not too expensive restaurant, the fourth place being made up by a lady in whom he had a genuine interest. It was a masterstroke. His matchmaking succeeded with almost indecent haste. The two were mainly in agreement but where they disagreed he would insist and she would coyly retreat. At modest cost Luke got rid of the unwanted lady, but she felt so guilty at having jilted him that he had ever since been able to call on her for favours, while the other luncheon-guest was so indignant at that treatment of him that she could refuse him nothing. It was one of those rare occasions on which everybody wins.

Audrey and her husband, as he became, had moved away to raise a family but they had returned to Birchgrove when the chicks left the nest. And now here she was in the nick of time, bringing the very qualities that the situation demanded.

A traffic policeman arrived, asking questions; but she sent him about his business, pointing out that it was an accident with nobody injured, the negligible damage to property was the business of the Canal Authority and Mr Grant's insurers and that she and Mr Grant would be available to make statements if these should ever prove necessary. She produced a mobile phone that was still dry and working and phoned Ledbetter to bring his recovery vehicle, extract the Land Rover from the canal, convey it to his garage and report to Mr Grant on the cause of the brake failure and whether the vehicle was repairable. In about five words she dismissed the lady with the perambulator – who was inclined to make a fuss, if not about the wetting then about

Luke's provocative remark. Luke was then loaded into the front seat of a respectable Honda, with a plastic mackintosh to protect the upholstery.

The Honda sailed up the steep hill in comparative silence. Luke, whose ears were tuned to elderly Land Rovers, was impressed. When, as they neared his house, Audrey learned that he had been on his way to visit his damaged granddaughter-in-law in Edinburgh, she announced that she would wait in the car while he changed into dry clothes and convey him there. From her reluctance to enter his house, it seemed that a resumption of their earlier relations was not on the cards. Luke, who had been thinking about a hire car but had lost his confidence and was reluctant to drive again so soon after such a fright, was relieved on both counts. He accepted gratefully.

A quick shower seemed to be called for, but while standing under the hot spray Luke became aware of pain in his left ankle – pain that he had had no spare mental capacity to recognize until it worsened as he began to calm down and the adrenaline cleared from his bloodstream. By the time he had dressed himself appropriately for hospital visiting he found it necessary to wind a crepe bandage around the foot and ankle and to finish, fumbling in haste, with a bedroom slipper. The picture was completed when he hobbled out to the car leaning on a heavy stick with an antler handle, a present from a gamekeeper for whom he had doctored some wildlife photographs.

He need not have hurried. Audrey was sound asleep, leaning back against the headrest. Luke was reminded that another reason for their parting company was that she was a mighty snorer and inclined to dribble. She roused on his approach, dabbed at her mouth and blinked at him.

He made it as far as the front passenger's door and answered her unspoken question. 'I must have wrenched my ankle during the crash,' he said. 'I didn't feel it until now.'

'That's sometimes the way with sprains. We can call at the surgery.'

'I think,' he said slowly, 'that my errand may be more urgent and I don't believe that delaying treatment will do my ankle any harm. If it gets too bad I can go into A and E.'

'Very well. It's your ankle.' He arranged

himself carefully. Audrey was a good driver, covering the road in good time, insisting on her right of way but without jerking him around. Even so, his ankle was beginning to pound. He distracted himself by looking for all the sights that a passenger may see but the driver misses.

'Do you think your granddaughter-in-law will be able to tell you who knocked her down?' Audrey asked suddenly. They were crossing the top of the Lammermuirs, the bleakness softened by the summer sun.

Luke was jerked out of his contemplation of the photographic potential of a stone bridge. 'How did you know—

She laughed. 'It's all over the place that you're asking questions. So you think the police are too easily satisfied?'

A bright and shining vintage car passed in the opposite direction. He turned his head, using it as an excuse to pause while he chose his words.

'I don't think anything of the sort,' he said at last. 'But I do know that they're busy. Also that they have other cases in which the criminal nature is more certain and they seem to be concentrating on those. This may have been a hit-and-run, which to my mind is wicked but understandable. It takes strength of mind to own up after a genuine accident. On the other hand, it may have been a deliberate attack – impulsive but evil all the same. To satisfy my own mind, I'm wondering who she'd quarrelled with and where everybody was on Friday night.'

She was giving due attention to her driving and it was some seconds before she spoke again. 'Why do you call it impulsive?'

The question was a challenge. Luke gave some thought to his reply. Any loose thinking would be jumped on and picked over. 'It would be a very uncertain place to lie in wait,' he said. 'Late though it was, a lot of functions happen on a Friday night and there would be people heading for home. A vehicle waiting in the open, or in one of the garages with the door up, would be remembered. Then again, from what the police inspector said, the vehicle must have hit and crushed her in reverse gear. That would be very difficult to do on purpose but very easy to do accidentally. The older Land Rovers don't have very good close-to rear vision.'

The discussion lapsed while she waited for traffic to escape from behind an artic. When it had cleared and they were bowling along

144

again she said, 'I'll accept that for the moment. Geoffrey and I had been shopping in Edinburgh. We called in on Hilda and Brian – our daughter and son-in-law, remember? – for a drink before starting for home. But we were home by ten thirty and in bed by eleven.' At the mention of bed she delivered an arch look through the driving mirror. 'As for quarrels, Mrs Highsmith is a touchy character. We got on well enough, usually.' (You would, Luke thought. Birds of a feather.) 'But she always wanted to argue even when she must have known that she didn't have a leg to stand on. We didn't really quarrel but there were a number of times when we had to agree to disagree.'

'For instance?'

'Political correctness, for one. She refuses to accept that there are some things that just have to be true if we're to make any progress, so we mustn't do or say anything to keep alive what has to be dead, whatever the reality may be. To her mind, using political correctness to justify saying something that you can't back up any other way is next to a lie. You understand?'

'I understand,' Luke said. For once he felt some sympathy with his granddaughter-in-law's attitude. Political correctness, being an assumption that the speaker knows best, always put his back up. 'As to whether she'll be able to tell me who did it, that depends. I don't suppose she saw who the driver was, in the dark and from behind. And even if she did so, whether she'll remember and ever be able to tell us … who knows?'

The rest of the journey was passed in silence with only occasional exchanges of trifling conversation. It was as if they had already strayed too close to dangerous ground. She pulled up at last outside the gates of the New Royal. 'I'm not going into the car parks,' she said. 'Do you know what they charge you now, even for the first ten seconds?' She dug into a handbag and produced a small card. 'Take this. It has my mobile number on it. I'm going to go and do some shopping. Phone me on my mobile and let me know when you're going to be ready to come home.'

She dropped him outside the main entrance and drove around the circuit to find a way out. Another woman in a BMW tried to force an entry into the stream of traffic but backed off when she saw that Audrey had no intention of giving way. Luke rather thought that she might have let a male driver in. He hobbled inside. Somebody tried to direct him to A and E but he took an uneasiness in his bowels to be an intuition that his errand was more urgent than mere pain. Or it might have been a telepathic message, or mere hunger.

He found himself in a long and lofty entrance hall. People were bustling or hobbling past, apparently confident where to go, but he was totally disoriented. He approached the main desk for directions. The New Edinburgh Royal Infirmary is built low so that he only had to go up one floor. Judging from the height of the hall, he guessed that the stairs would be a challenge for his hips and knees and even more so for his ankle. He took a lift and then limped endlessly.

He found the right nursing station at last. The ward sister was profoundly relieved to see him. 'We've been waiting for you,' she said.

'Why on earth?'

'Mrs Highsmith was very woozy as she first woke up but as her mind cleared she became agitated. She wasn't fit to use the phone so she persuaded me to call her lawyer. He's with her now. I've tried again to reach you. I was just going to try again when you arrived.'

'My mobile suffered in the same accident as my ankle did.' Luke bit off his questions. There was no point asking the sister what he would be able to ask Emily. He let her lead him into a small room or large cubicle where monitors, watched by a very young-looking nurse, were registering all Emily's bodily functions. Emily lay, pale and heavily bandaged, but at least there was no longer a tent over her.

Beside the cot, Mr Enterkin slouched in an unsuitable chair, apparently dozing but with an A4 pad on his knee. He was the premier local solicitor round about Newton Lauder, despite being very nearly Luke's age. He had retired at least once but, having been fetched out of retirement to deal with the aftermath of a case that he had fought and won, he found, by the time that he had wound it up, that other matters had arrived on his desk that his secretary had been too tender-hearted to turn away. He was relieved. He had not enjoyed retirement.

He snorted, grunted and awoke as Luke sat down. After some seconds he recalled where he was and who Luke happened to be. 'At last!' he said – very quietly as befitted the place and despite his obvious irritation. 'We've been trying your mobile phone number over and over. If you have one of those infernal contraptions you could at least switch it on.'

'I did,' Luke told him. 'Unfortunately my Land Rover suffered brake failure and went into the canal and my mobile was drowned.'

That, along with the stick and the bandage, rather took the wind out of the solicitor's sails but he was spared the need to reply because Emily stirred, gasped and woke. Her hand went immediately to the release of the on-demand painkiller and in a few more seconds the obvious signs of pain abated. Her eyes still failed to focus, but evidently her ears were working. 'Is that you, GG?' she asked in little more than a whisper.

'It is.' He was struggling to formulate an enquiry after her well-being that wouldn't be too stupid in the circumstances when she spoke again.

'They say that I'll have to have more operations. I didn't understand it all, but I believe they've fixed most of my bones but a lot of my insides are damaged. It certainly feels like that. GG, I don't think I'm going to make it.'

Luke looked quickly at the nurse but she avoided his eye. 'Of course you will!' he said. 'I always knew that you could do anything that you really wanted to do. Listen. Did you see who was driving the other vehicle?'

'No idea and it doesn't matter a damn now. What's the point of revenge? There are much more important things to be dealt with. You listen to me. I made a will some time ago, leaving everything to you in trust for the girls. It isn't a lot but if you sell the house...'

'Is there nobody more suitable in the longer term?'

She tried to shake her head but the effort was too much. 'Nobody, GG.' She sounded closer to tears than he had ever heard in her voice. 'I don't respect you. I don't even like you. But I trust you as I don't trust anyone else. So I want you to be a father to the girls instead of a great-grandfather. I got poor Mr Enterkin here to draw up some papers, just to be sure that those idiots in the Social Services don't get a bee in their bonnets about suitability and so on.'

Mr Enterkin laid his pad on the bed. It was patterned with his very precise writing. 'It's all in manuscript,' he said, 'but perfectly legal for all that. If you both sign it in front of witnesses and add the words "Adopted as holograph", that will be all that's necessary – assuming, of course, that Mrs Highsmith is correct in her prognostication. I take it that you're willing to undertake the responsibility?'

'Yes, of course. They're my direct descendants. How could I not?'

'When Violet reaches twenty-one,' Emily whispered, 'she will take over responsibility for Jane.'

The quiet was broken by voices and a clatter of feet as a trolley went past in a hurry, bearing a still figure.

'You do both realize that I'm over eighty?' Luke asked. 'How can you be sure that I'll live that long?'

Emily managed a faint chuckle. 'Been watching you for years,' she whispered. 'Mean and stubborn, like me, and as fit as a flea. If you can't take it with you, you won't go.'

'That does sound rather like me,' he

admitted. Her sight seemed to be improving so he let her see that he was smiling. 'Violet and Jane show signs of the same determination. But, Emily, are you physically capable of signing?'

She raised her right arm. It was bruised but otherwise undamaged. Luke went to the nurses' station and fetched the ward sister. She and the nurse acted as witnesses and the business was soon completed.

'Do you want anything else?' he asked Emily.

'Nothing. I couldn't eat fruit, and flowers give me asthma. I don't want to be visited yet and I don't want the girls to see me at all. I'd only give them nightmares. When I pop off, do what you bloody like, but if you want to respect my wishes they are that I wouldn't want a lot of fuss and flap and hymn-singing and people saying hypocritical things about me. But do what you like, say what you like and have a party if you want to, it'll be all the same to me. Just remember that I don't want to clutter up the ground. Cremation and dig the ashes into your garden or let them blow into the face of that damn-fool minister. That's all. You can both bugger off now. I want to sleep again.' She closed her eyes and seemed to drift away.

Mr Enterkin was preparing to rise. He was reputed to be the slowest driver north of the Wash, but that suited Luke's mood for the moment. 'Can I beg a lift back to Newton Lauder?' Luke asked.

'Certainly.'

'You wouldn't happen to have a mobile phone?'

'Again, certainly. I do not approve of them, in fact I hate them with a deadly hatred, but I find mine indispensable.'

The nurse looked up from the instrumentation. 'You mustn't use a mobile phone in here,' she said. 'It can interfere with the instrumentation and pacemakers and ... and that sort of thing.'

'Young woman,' said Mr Enterkin, 'you should learn to listen to what is being said rather than what you think is being said. Mr Grant did not ask for my phone, he merely enquired as to whether I had one of the abominable instruments. We can phone from my car. That will do?' he enquired.

'I only want to tell my lift that I shan't need her services again. She won't have had time to finish her shopping,' said Luke. He moved towards giving Emily a kiss on the forehead but the nurse frowned at him. Sterility, of course. Anyway, her eyes had already closed. He told her that he would see her again, without having the faintest idea as to whether it would be true or even whether she could hear him. It was with great relief that he escaped from the mingled atmospheres of doom and dogoodery and production-line repair.

'Can you wait a minute or two while I get something done about this ankle? If they can't see me straight away I'll come out again and you can drop me at the surgery in Newton Lauder.'

'Very well,' said Mr Enterkin. 'But I'll come in with you and if you can't get seen straight away I'll call your lift to pick you up here and be on my way.'

Nine

Mr Enterkin waited, but without showing signs of patience, while Luke paid a call in A and E. He could normally have feared a lengthy wait and he would have had to let his choice of lifts go, but the first person to glance at his ankle for purposes of triage was a competent young lady who bandaged it more professionally, gave him a painkiller and sent him on his way to make room for the more seriously injured.

Luke soon accepted that Mr Enterkin's reputation as a slow driver was, if anything, understated. He was tempted to borrow the other's mobile phone, to phone Audrey Shanks again and countermand his previous call. She could, he estimated, have overtaken them before they were clear of the outskirts of Edinburgh. But he was tired after a day of excitements and the warmth and sunlight of the day seemed to encourage somnolence.

He leaned back in the very comfortable seats and closed his eyes. The document that he had just signed required a little thought. He intended to think but very soon he was asleep.

They were approaching the turnoff for Newton Lauder when he was awoken by the increasing pain in his ankle, but otherwise much refreshed. He had just got out of the solicitor's car at Ledbetter's garage when Audrey's car pulled up beside him. The driver's window wound itself down. 'They won't have one to drive away,' she said.

'I can get his taxi to take me home.'

'I'll wait for you,' she said in a tone that did not invite argument. Mr Enterkin gave him a man-to-man wink and drove off.

Ledbetter's garage and service station stood by the main road into Newton Lauder from the north, fronted by several fuel pumps under a sheltering canopy and a short row of highly polished vehicles for sale, mostly trade-ins. Behind the gaudy bulk of the garage was another, only slightly smaller but considerably less neat and businesslike. This had been the original garage. Here Ledbetter Junior worked his magic on clapped-out Land Rovers. A row of those and similar jeep-type vehicles, carefully arranged with the more seemly examples placed where the passing public could see them, were graduated along the row to the utterly decrepit and, tucked away at the least conspicuous end, those that had already been partially cannibalised to provide parts for others.

Inside the wooden shed were a Land Rover and a Shogun, each in process of restoration, and Luke's Land Rover still dripping canal water onto the otherwise clean concrete floor. There was a strong smell of cough-drops that Luke recognized as being from the cellulose spray paint that Ledbetter Junior used, always in olive green irrespective of whatever colour the vehicle might have been when delivered to him.

Ledbetter Junior put down the spray gun, pushed up his facemask and shook his head sadly. 'A write-off,' he said sadly, nodding towards Luke's vehicle. 'No doubt about it. Gearbox and transfer box wrecked and crankcase cracked. The chassis, which was well rusted, seems to have got a twist at the same time. Not economically repairable. I'll give you a report for your insurers.'

Although when away from his business

premises young Ledbetter was a very shy man, inclined to fall over his feet when spoken to, he was just as big a crook as any other motor dealer. Luke suspected that if he bought a replacement and left his old friend with Ledbetter to be broken, he would see most of it running around the neighbourhood within a few months. But it would be the insurance company, if anybody, that would be robbed if Ledbetter could get away with it.

Luke had a good idea of what he wanted. Times were becoming hostile to four-by-fours that drank almost as much fuel as a government limo, but to pursue his profession he did need to have access to remote corners of Scotland. For that purpose he required four-wheel drive and a good ground clearance. He had just received payment for a photo-shoot on Crete and there was more to come. During the photo-shoot the supermodel had almost been sent home because her pregnancy was beginning to show. Luke had saved the day by offering to correct her silhouette on the computer. The contract on which he always insisted would permit him to sell the uncorrected shots to the magazines at a later date. News of an unmarried supermodel's pregnancy with photographs, along with library shots of the three different men each claiming to be the father and one who denied paternity despite her insistent claims, would definitely sell. He pointed to the Daihatsu Terios at the superior end of the line. 'How much, really?'

'The price is on it.'

'Now let's have a good laugh and start again.'

Ledbetter Junior smiled winningly. 'Would you like a test drive?'

Luke leaned heavily on his stick. His ankle was beginning to hurt worse. He was tempted to accept the test drive for the sake of sitting down, but the vehicle was very neat and clean and time was beginning to press. 'I don't need a test drive. That's the car that Johnny Friel traded in because he needed more carrying capacity. I rode in it with him last week. I want that small dent in the rear wing removed and the radio changed to one that has a CD player with a stacking magazine. You keep my Land Rover. You can show the insurance company any figures you like, the bottom line is how much do you want, and think you can get, from me for the swap?'

They talked figures while Audrey sat peacefully in her car on the forecourt. Tired from taking his weight on one leg, Luke leaned against the Terios and damned the dust transferring to his pale trousers. They reached agreement although it would take Ledbetter two days to modify the car and license it for the road. Luke phoned his insurers from the office. Once the deal was confirmed Ledbetter said, 'You'd better mind your back. Or call the police. Or both. Looked to me like your brake-pipes had been cut, and the handbrake cables too.'

Luke absorbed the news without showing any reaction. Land Rovers and crime had been juxtaposed in his thoughts for several days. 'I'll tell the police. You say nothing to anybody.'

'If that's the way you want it.'

'It is.'

Luckily, Luke's smallest digital camera had been in his shirt pocket and had emerged undamaged. His mobile phone had not been so lucky. He allowed Audrey to drive him to the shop where, in addition to TVs and video recorders, mobile phones could be bought. He was in luck. The proprietor had a 'Pay as you Go' phone available. Luke bought it on the spot and, as soon as Audrey had dropped him at his own door, he hobbled inside and phoned Helena's number to let the girls know that he was home.

He heard Helena's car minutes later and the girls arrived, bursting with news of their day, but they found him on the phone again, this time to his service provider in order to get his old number transferred to his new phone. Pepper fussed around his feet. Luke told all of them to be very careful of his bad ankle.

As soon as he had managed to find his way through the red tape, the babble broke over him. 'How was Mum? Helena's planting a row of fuschias ... What happened to your ankle? Pepper told us you were back, before your phone call ... What colour will the fuschias be? Where's your Land Rover? When's Mum coming home? How does Pepper know you're back while you're still half a mile away?'

He gave them an answer about their mother without really telling them anything and told them all about his accident with the exception of Ledbetter's report. 'I'll have another car quite soon,' he said. 'Until then, I'm stuck. And it hurts me to stand for long. So can I count on you two to help out with the housework and cooking?'

The two girls exchanged a look. 'Provided you tell us exactly how to do it,' Violet said. Jane nodded. Most teenagers would have asked what was in it for them, but Luke noted with delight the ready acceptance.

'I suppose you wouldn't be hungry just now?' Luke said.

'Yes we would,' Jane protested.

'She's always hungry,' Violet explained.

'Well, I only had a sandwich out of a machine instead of lunch and I could eat either or both of you unsalted, so let's get going.' Luke's mouth began to water at the thought of food. 'I'll hop or hobble through and sit on the stool in the kitchen and conduct the gastronomic orchestra from there. I'll show you how to do a really good steak and chips. But first you go upstairs and make sure that your rooms are really, truly, properly tidy and bring down the laundry basket and anything that needs washing. It's time that I introduced you to the mysteries of laundry programs. I am not, repeat not, going to wash your smalls for you.'

'But we have to wash yours?' said Jane.

'Now you're getting the idea.'

As soon as Jane had thundered up the stairs, followed more decorously by her sister, Luke phoned the police headquarters and left a message to the effect that Detective Inspector Fellowes should pay him a call as soon as possible in order to gather the latest news. After that, he settled down to jotting down the numbers that he wanted programmed into his new mobile phone. The shop had been able to provide him with a booklet of user's instructions for a not quite identical model, but these seemed to have been translated almost literally from the Japanese by somebody not wholly familiar with either language. What was needed for such a task was an intelligent ten-year-old and Jane would do very nicely.

Detective Inspector Ian Fellowes arrived next morning while the girls were out walking Pepper and doing the dogging-in. Young girls take readily to dog handling and Pepper had taken to the girls. Luke was sitting on the kitchen stool and washing the breakfast dishes. His ankle was more swollen and very painful. The day was fine and the front door stood open, so Luke was able to invite the DI in without getting off the stool.

The DI settled himself in a kitchen chair and nodded towards Luke's bandage. 'I heard about your dive into the canal,' he said. 'Was this an outcome of it?'

'Presumably.' Luke dried the last plate. 'I didn't feel it at the time, thanks, I suppose, to the adrenaline rush, but it's been getting worse. If I had a car I'd go to the surgery.'

Ian Fellowes had been holding himself upright, maintaining his official aspect, but he relaxed a little and even half-smiled. 'All right. I can take a hint. I have my own car outside. But only as far as the surgery, mind. If they want you to go into Edinburgh for an X-ray or a scan they can send you in an ambulance. And you make your own way home. What was it you were going to tell me?'

Luke gave the worktop a final wipe and turned round to face the room but he stayed on his stool. 'According to Mr Ledbetter – the younger one – my brake-pipes and cables had been cut. I told him to save the wreck for you. When you manage to clear your feet of all the break-ins, assaults and thefts from washing lines you might care to consider a matter of attempted murder.'

Ian Fellowes was looking tired but he

managed another smile. 'You have no call to feel bitter,' he said. 'All we had – indeed, all we still have – was or is a case of serious injury by motor car, which might have been no more than an accident and a guilty driver driving away out of fear of the consequences. But much has changed. Thanks to a little luck and some brilliant detective work, we've reduced the unsolved cases to what my small force can manage. So I'm turning my attention back to you. If you hadn't phoned me I was going to come to you anyway.

'Sudden and complete brake failure isn't that common and certainly adds a touch of verisimilitude. More often it happens progressively. The brake pedal feels soft but you can pump the pedal and get some braking. A competent driver using his gearbox can usually bleed off the rest of his speed.'

There are certain activities about which the average male resents criticism, direct or oblique. Driving comes second or third on the list. Also resented is having one's words of wisdom turned back against one. 'I'll have you know, Inspector,' Luke said hotly, 'that despite the steepness of the hill I used my gearbox until both it and the transfer box gave way. Of course, the engine stopped dead and I lost the power steering straight away. It was like steering a battleship except that a battleship probably has featherlight steering powered by a huge diesel. After that, there was nothing that anyone could have done except to try to avoid hitting anyone else and to aim for a soft landing, both of which I achieved.'

DI Fellowes did not look in the least abashed. 'Well, bully for you! I'll go down and take a look. Perhaps young Ledbetter's going off half-cocked, but perhaps not. It can sometimes be difficult to tell the difference. How is Mrs Highsmith?'

It occurred to Luke that nobody had given him a proper medical report on his granddaughter-in-law's condition. He chose his words carefully. 'She's had major surgery but there's more to come,' he said. 'When I saw her, she was very weak but her mind was all there. She had fetched Mr Enterkin through at the same time and they had me sign something that makes me responsible for the girls. Emily doesn't think she's going to make it and, frankly, those who contradict her do so without a great deal of conviction so I don't know. I've been formally appointed trustee and guardian until she's fit again or Violet's old enough to take over, whichever comes first. I asked her, on behalf of the young copper at her bedside, whether she saw the driver but she says not. Well, if a Land Rover is reversing towards you in darkness – and it had to be reversing, to judge from the height of her injuries – you probably won't see the driver except possibly as a vague shape through the rear window, silhouetted against the lights if there's anything for them to shine on. You told me that she was carrying a carton of supplies. If the other vehicle had been facing towards her, the carton would have been all or mostly above the level of the bonnet and the nudge bar. Her injuries would have been to her legs and abdomen, not to her torso.'

DI Fellowes was usually more forthcoming than most policemen, but he made no comment on Luke's observations. 'What, if anything, have you heard that might suggest the identity of the driver?' he asked.

'On the wall of my workroom, opposite the door, there's a sheet of paper with writing on it. If you fetch it through I'll explain it to you.' Ian Fellowes got up. 'And while you're on your feet,' Luke added, 'perhaps you'd hang this on the towel-rail.'

The DI took the damp dishtowel and hung it over the heated towel-rail. Muttering something about opportunism and a bloody nerve, he went through to Luke's workroom. Luke gave some thought to the inspector's calumny on his driving. Had it been a piece of verbal clumsiness or had he intended to provoke Luke into being more outspoken and perhaps not thinking about what he said?

Ian Fellowes came back with the paper. Luke left his stool, made one hop to the table and took a chair. 'All the residents of Birchgrove are here in the left-hand column,' he said. 'There are also a few outsiders whose names happened to come up. I couldn't take in the whole of Newton Lauder, but it makes much more sense to consider this the work of a local rather than an outsider lying in wait.

'The next column is for quarrels that I have been told about, between Emily and the people on the first list. You may as well ignore it as far as it's gone. None of them seem to be enough to provoke such a drastic action but Emily is undoubtedly a very quarrelsome person. I was going to mark the quarrels from one to ten, but who knows how seriously somebody else may take a given insult? One lady insists that the insult was so appalling that she still can't repeat it, but it may turn out to be an allegation that she picks her nose or something equally trifling. Just how my grandson managed to put up with Emily I don't know. Perhaps she was outstanding in the marital bed.'

'Or perhaps she brought some money with her.'

'That's possible,' Luke said, much taken with the idea. He hoped very hard that it was correct. His great-granddaughters might soon have to fend for themselves but cash for dowries or other extravagances would smooth their paths. 'Anyway, she never hesitated before picking a quarrel with absolutely anybody, so I don't think that you'll find much guidance there. Neither I nor any of my spies has come across any other motive. The remaining column is given over to who is known to have been elsewhere at the time.'

The DI nodded. 'Commonly but colloquially known as alibis?'

'Yes. Luckily, Friday nights are the active night around here and that night more than most. Those marked A were at a darts match at the Canal Bar. Those with a B were at a bridge tournament. The Cs were at dinner at Hay Lodge. That's as far as I've been able to go.'

'But it may have been far enough for somebody to see – or imagine – that you were getting close to evidence of attempted murder.' The DI straightened up from his perusal of Luke's chart and met his eye. 'Or have you made any enemies who would like to see the back of you? An angry husband? A slighted lady-friend?'

Luke felt himself grow hot. He drew himself up as far as he could while sitting in a hard and upright chair. 'Inspector,' he said, 'there is no way that a normal, single man could live so close to that ... that hot-bed of widows and divorcees and not have the occasional affair, unless he was prepared to bolt like a rabbit any time that a lovely lady gave him the come-on which, frankly, I was not – at least until recently.' He paused to draw a fresh breath. 'But I can honestly say that there are no aggrieved husbands and that I am still on good terms with any lady who ever had a ... a relationship with me. You can ask any of them.'

'I can?'

Luke realized that such permission might entail the preparation of a list and the betrayal of some tender secrets. 'No,' he said. 'Perhaps not. But it's true all the same.'

'Then you'd better tell me what has come out of your researches so far.'

Luke shrugged. 'You can hardly draw a firm conclusion from purely negative data,' he said, 'but so far I can only suggest that you take a good, hard look at those people who are not alibied by events in the third column. There are twenty-two of those, counting only the adults, comprising six couples and ten singletons. Two of the couples are very old. You may find that some of the singletons were avoiding the Friday night events and staying at home in order to visit each other or to child-sit for neighbours, so there may be more alibis to come.'

The DI was running his finger down the third column and then across to read the corresponding names. Something seemed to be perturbing him, but before Luke could get around to ask him what was getting up his nose they were interrupted by the arrival of the two girls, full of excitement over a morning that had been both fun and useful

– a combination that they had never previously experienced.

'GG,' Jane burst out, 'Pepper's a girl-dog, isn't she?'

'A bitch. Yes.'

'When she has puppies, can I have one?'

'She won't be having any more puppies,' Luke said. 'She's been spayed.' Jane's face fell. Luke had been thinking of starting a new puppy in order to have a successor when Pepper came to the end of her days but he had decided that it would not be fair to a pup to take it on while knowing that his own active years were numbered. But here was a solution being presented to him. 'If you two can show me that you can look after Pepper, keep up the training and feeding and brushing and searching for ticks, I'll get a puppy for you to train and walk and you two can keep it when I get too old. Mr Calder was talking about putting his Muttley to stud.'

Jane ran outside, shrieking with delight, but Violet was suddenly brought to the realisation that her great-grandfather was not immortal. Her eyes became moist. 'GG, are you all right?'

'Barring old age, yes. Why?'

'It can't be easy, limping on both feet.' She studied his face, looking for signs of decrepitude; but her inspection was evidently satisfactory because she blinked, forced a smile and followed her sister outside.

'Lovely girls,' the detective inspector said absently. He had spent the period of the interruption in further study of Luke's chart. 'As you quite correctly hinted, the rest of the work is mine. The presence or absence of alibis is a notoriously uncertain starting-point but it seems to be all that we have. Even so there is one enquiry ... quite a simple one really ... but an enquiry that I have a personal reason...'

The DI's hesitant words petered out.

'If you're working round to asking me to pursue another enquiry for you,' Luke said, 'you'd better come out with it. I may be inclined to help. But do remember that I'm not fleet of foot at the moment and I may be without a car for a few more days.'

'I hadn't forgotten, believe me. But, if anything, it helps. You seem to know them both, so it would not be unreasonable to beg a lift off them. I'm referring to Joline Henderson and Mary Kemp, single ladies sharing a house. They had some trouble recently with

173

some very offensive anonymous letters. There have been recurrent rumours about them being lesbians.' The inspector flushed slightly and scratched his chin. 'I went to see them about the letters. I had it firmly in my head that there was some truth behind the letters ... because of what somebody had said only that morning ... and when they suggested that the letters were coming from a disgruntled ex-boyfriend I let my surprise show. In fact ... I forget my exact words ... but I could have expressed myself more tactfully.'

'In other words, you put your foot in it.'

The detective inspector turned pink. 'You could put it that way. They hit the ceiling and ordered me out of the house. Anyway, they left me in no doubt that any further approaches from me, even with the weight of the law on my side, would not be welcome. And I can hardly send one of my own men. God knows what they'd say to him.'

'You don't have a woman officer in your team?'

'Not one that I could trust not to have a giggle at my expense.'

With some reluctance, Luke promised that he would try to sound them out.

The inspector had another call to make but would come back. Luke put his foot up on a second chair and rested for a minute while he let his mind drift back. A new garden centre had been opening up in Newton Lauder. Luke had taken the PR photographs and was invited to the opening ceremony and party. Tired after walking round the beds of plants and standing making conversation, he had subsided onto one of the chairs arranged round the walls of what was to become the sales hall. He was soon rested and thinking about replenishing his glass, so he put a hand on the adjoining chair seat to help himself up. As he did so, a lady in a thin summer dress sat down on his hand. She jumped up and apologized.

Luke had had a few drinks and he was slightly fuddled. 'No need to apologize,' he replied. 'You're welcome to...' He had got so far before he realized where his sentence was irrevocably leading. He broke off, struggling to think of a conclusion to the sentence that did not seem to be expressing pleasure at having his hand sat on. But the woman was ahead of him. Instead of being offended, she produced a loud but not unmusical laugh that stopped conversations across the crowded room.

Joline Henderson was resident in Birchgrove. He had seen her once or twice in the shops and had admired her figure. Her figure was certainly open to admiration. It did not emulate a stick insect, like that of many a contemporary model, but instead was formed of exquisitely perfect curves, rounded and flowing into each other as intended by a benevolent nature. After such an introduction it was not surprising that she was soon his mistress although, having a home less than a mile away, she never moved out of the house that she shared with Mary Kemp.

Unfortunately Joline's face did not live up to her figure. She looked, in fact, rather like the better sort of bulldog. Mary Kemp was an artist, producing a broad range of illustrations for magazines and book-jackets. Joline scraped a living as a model for Mary and other artists. It is little or no trouble to an artist to graft a different head onto a body, and Mary herself was the perfect counterpart to Joline, having a well-shaped skull and a face of quite angelic beauty framed by a mop of golden hair, set on top of an ill-proportioned body. With the arrival of digital photography it had become just as easy for the photographer to carry out a head transplant without surgery and later, when called on for glamour photography, Luke often made use of the two as models.

It took only ten days of the romance between Luke and Joline for him to find that she was not his ideal. Her idea of sexual union was to close her eyes, lie back and wait passively for an orgasm to arrive. Some of her friends addressed her as Joy and this he found perfectly apt. She was often tired at night and wanted only to sleep but usually woke with her appetite and energy freshly aroused. The psalm assures us that 'Joy cometh in the morning,' and Luke decided that the psalmist must have known somebody exactly like Joline.

Beneath a glib and superficial gloss of sophistication there was no intelligence at all. Conversation with Joline, he found, was the counterpart to her attitude to sex. Thoughts of a kind washed around in her head but she had not the remotest idea of sorting the wheat from the chaff and such thoughts as she decided to express seemed to require an inordinate number of words.

Several times he asked her to skip to the punch line and only then, if at all, fill in the background; but he was met by a blank stare and another outpouring. Rather than give way to impulse and say 'For God's sake shut up,' his only recourse was to let words flow past him while he thought about something else. As long as he nodded and smiled occasionally she suspected nothing.

Other men, he knew, had adopted the same habit, but it was not one that he relished. As it turned out, her affection was little engaged if at all, and when Luke at last suggested that he did not feel like availing himself of her body any more she nodded, smiled and went off to look for somebody else. They had remained friends.

Joline had put up a successful defence against the passing of time and exercised regularly at the gym in order to keep her perfect curves in perfect trim. Luke continued to use her body for photographic purposes, often allied to Mary's head, whenever glamour was required.

His reverie was brought to an end by a tooting in the track outside. The DI had returned. Luke explained quickly to his great-granddaughters just how he would like them to behave during his absence, with particular emphasis on housework, and limped out into the sunshine. He could hear the start of a ball game before even closing the door of the DI's car.

Ten

The local medical practice was headed by Dr Charlotte Gowans. The doctor was a plump and silver-haired lady now due for retirement but Luke still attended her surgery when he was in need of attention – which, considering his years, was mercifully rare. She had been his doctor ever since she graduated and she knew his case history. In fact, Luke felt that she knew rather more than was proper of the case histories of the locals. On one occasion she had sent off a sample of his blood to be tested in connection with a stomach infection. In giving him the result she had also given him a pointed look as she remarked that, 'They also found traces of thrush.' Luke had not seen the significance of the remark until after he had left the surgery or the embarrassment that he suffered might have been even more acute. Thrush, he was sure, was a woman's disease. As to how it could have been passed to him and what deductions the doctor might have made, he closed his mind.

Her manner remained wholly professional as she examined his ankle and put a fresh bandage around it. In her opinion it was rather more than a bad sprain. She gave him two prescriptions and told him to rest it and phone her in a week if it was not substantially better. Before he left she said, 'You've been prone to trouble in that leg. It comes from favouring the other leg because of your damaged foot. We don't want this injury to become permanent. One of those prescriptions is for Capsaicin, for rubbing in. The active ingredient is the same as in chilli peppers, so wash your hands immediately afterwards. In particular, don't touch your eyes or any sores or tender places or you'll go through the roof. Remember, now.'

'I'll remember.'

As soon as he had hobbled outside, Luke used his mobile phone. Mary Kemp answered the call so he asked for Joline. Joy, Mary said, was doing some shopping. She answered on her mobile at the second ring.

Perfect!

Joline, it appeared, already knew about his accident and the injured ankle. She had happened upon the scene while his Land Rover was being extricated from the canal and had been concerned enough to make enquiries. She would be happy to give him transport. She picked him up from outside the surgery, asked after Helena's state of health and then settled into talk mode. She drove an almost unscratched and dent-free Land Rover competently and with confidence. Whether her mind was on her driving or what she was saying, or neither, baffled him. When she was about to sweep past the short cut into Birchgrove he had to interrupt in the middle of the story of her encounter with somebody who Luke had never met, complete with a word perfect reiteration of every word that each participant had thought or spoken. 'Would you take me to your house, please? I want a word with you and Mary together.'

Joline barely paused in her discourse but she slowed and in two brisk hand movements and a foot pressure she was in a low gear and four-wheel drive and bumping up the almost impossible back road to Birchgrove. 'What was I saying?'

Luke had not been listening. 'You were telling me what you said to her,' he said. It was a safe bet. Deftly, Joline picked up the subject, only to break off at her own front door.

'I can carry something for you, if it's light,' Luke said.

She laughed. 'Bless you, no need! Go on in.' She gathered up half a dozen carrier bags by the handles. Under her perfect figure there must have been perfect musculature, because what must have been a considerable weight seemed to require no effort. Luke part-hopped and part-limped ahead and threw open the door for her. Joline dumped her parcels in the kitchen and then led the way through the house.

A useful small studio had been created by the erection of a large greenhouse, occupying most of the small back garden. All the glass except for the northern half of the roof had been replaced by plastic-covered insulation-board and in sunny weather a small air conditioner worked hard to hold the temperature down. Mary was at work on a drawing board propped up on an old-fashioned plan chest. She only spared him a glance when Luke arrived and looked over her shoulder. Her expression was one of terror, but Luke was not concerned. Mary was in the process of adding, in ink and watercolour, her own head, as viewed in the mirror standing behind the drawing board, to a body that could only have belonged to Joline. From the attitude of the figure and the expression on her face it was clear that she was being manhandled and this, in conjunction with the figure's state of partial undress, made the vignette highly erotic. Mary would never make a fortune as an artist but her line drawings were brilliant and she had a special knack for that sort of art.

A storyboard propped beside the mirror told, in a less talented hand, a tale of so-far unrequited lust. A quick glance told Luke rather more than he needed to know. The Joline character, largely disrobed and with her wrists tied, managed to escape from her ravisher into the countryside. She hid to avoid certain obviously disreputable characters and then sought the help of an apparently respectable gentleman who turned out to be the worst of the lot.

Mary relaxed, let out a long breath and laid down her brush. 'It's for an American porn magazine,' she said. 'It may not be great art but it pays well. I'll be needing a male model next. Fancy doing it, Luke? You have just the right sort of dangerous look about you and I could always knock off a few years. It pays, and you get to cuddle Joline in her undies.' She might have been speaking about the weather.

'No great novelty there,' Joline said. 'I'll go and put the kettle on.' The door closed softly behind her.

Several folding chairs stood against one of the walls. Luke pulled one of them out and settled into it. 'You make it sound very tempting,' he said, 'but it will be weeks before I can stand on this ankle for any length of time. And, as Joline said, it does rather lack the allure of novelty. If it had been you, though...'

Mary had picked up a pencil and was sketching in a little of the background. 'You old flatterer,' she said. 'What would Helena say?'

Luke told himself that he really must keep a guard on his tongue. That had been the sort of casual remark that had led him into mischief in the past. Not that he was averse to a little mischief, but now he had Helena to think about. And the two girls, he reminded himself. Emily must have been expecting him to set a good example, poacher turning gamekeeper. 'You have a point there,' he said, averting his eyes from the drawing. 'Why don't you try young Ledbetter? He has the right sort of look and I'll bet he'd be glad to escape from the Land Rovers for a while and get his hands on a girl instead.'

Mary produced a laugh that was very close to a giggle. 'That may be a good idea. I may call on him in the morning. Thank you, Luke. And, for another character, if I give you a sketch could you manage a photograph of yourself that I could work from? Time will be getting short soon and I prefer not to go to an agency.'

Joline called that there was tea in the pot. 'Coming,' Mary called back. She gave Luke a helpful pull to get him on his feet – a movement that he was finding very difficult with only a part of one working foot. The sitting room was small but made to seem larger by being uncluttered and by the use of pale, bluish colours and small, light furniture. Only the presence of people betrayed the scale. Half-drawn curtains kept the sunshine at arm's length.

Tea was served in delicate but generously sized Wedgwood and there were delicious small cakes. Luke had almost forgotten what a good cook Joline was.

'How was Emily?' Mary asked.

'Not good at all,' Luke said, 'and very despondent. She was so convinced that she was moribund that she had Mr Enterkin along to draw up deeds making me responsible for the girls. And, to save you asking, if she saw who ran her over she hasn't remembered it yet.'

'Memory usually returns,' Joline said. 'My brother fell off a roof and he couldn't remember anything about it for a fortnight. He was sure that I'd pushed him. And I hadn't.'

Mary's usually jolly prettiness had darkened. 'A terrible thing,' she said. 'And the police...?'

'Detective Inspector Fellowes is taking statements.' Luke was not at all sure how to word what next he had to say, so he listened with interest as his own voice went on. 'He was shy about approaching you himself in case you still were still uptight about his clumsy approach when he came to see you about something else.' There! That sounded all right.

Joline's usually smooth brow was furrowed. 'Did we quarrel with him the last time he was here? I'd forgotten.'

'We were only pulling his leg for believing that we're a couple of lezzies,' said Mary. 'Is he still scared to come near us?' She spluttered with laughter. 'That's too bad.'

'It is too bad,' Luke agreed, 'and it was too bad of you to leave the poor man thinking that you'd shout at him or lead him a dance if he came near you again. He asked me to find out where you were on Friday night.'

'As if we'd do anything to embarrass the poor man!' Mary said. 'I can tell you where we were easily enough. One of my friends, a one-time fellow student from art school, had a birthday party and we were invited. She lives in Gorebridge and we were there until almost one in the morning, so there are plenty of witnesses. You can tell the inspector that if he takes his courage in both hands and comes to see us we'll give him about twenty names of people who were there and we won't even pull his leg one little bit. And – listen – it was your granddaughter-in-law who was spreading the tale that we were gay, but we didn't hold it against her. Joline thought it was funny and I didn't even know about it until much later. Your Inspector Fellowes had a serious word with her about anonymous letters. She may not have been writing them but they stopped. So there!'

In his youth, Luke had had a sense of humour that sometimes ran away with him. The years had sobered him, but he still fell victim to mad impulses now and again. 'Pay the inspector back for what he thought about you,' he suggested. 'I'll try to warn you when he's on the way here. Have Joline prepared exactly how she is in your drawing. See if you get him to stand in, even just for a second or two. Say that it's just to give you the scale of the male figure. That'll scare him really witless.'

The ladies laughed. Joline said that she was game, but Mary's mind was elsewhere. 'You did know,' she said, 'that your grand-daughter-in-law had a boyfriend?'

It took Luke some seconds to adjust his mind to the possibility. In view of Emily's frequently expressed contempt for men it seemed unlikely, but when he came to think about it she was just as contemptuous of the women who fell for them. 'No, I didn't. It's the first I've heard of it. Who?'

'Now, that I can't tell you. Do you know, Joline?'

Joline perked up. Luke thought that she must feel starved of her share of the conversation. 'No idea. And I didn't particularly care except that she was trying to keep it a deathly secret so I was saving it up to make her squirm next time she looked down her nose at us. It was Marigold Hicks who told me. She seemed absolutely certain so I suppose it's true, but can you really believe what you hear from a woman who's named after a pair of rubber gloves?'

The question seemed to be rhetorical, so Luke ignored it. Marigold Hicks had acquired a husband who was eternally suspicious, which added to his desire to meet her on neutral territory. 'Do me another favour,' he said. 'Ring her up. If she's at home, ask her to step round here for a minute.'

There had been an earlier occasion when Luke had attended a function and found that almost every one of his former loves was present, mostly with husbands in attendance. All eyes had seemed to be on him like angry little hands, and principally on his trousers. Pure coincidence had been at work, as he proved to himself later, although until he got over the first shock he had suspected a malignant practical joke or possibly an edition of *This Is Your Life*.

As they waited for Marigold Hicks to arrive, he experienced much the same feeling. How was it that almost every potential witness to his granddaughter-in-law's accident had at one time been a visitor to his bed? But the answer was only too obvious. He had been a widower now for more than 40 years. In this rather liberated, female-dominated enclave it was inevitable that eyes would be turned towards him from time to time and he had never been famous for his resistance to temptation. Even at one a year – and there was no doubt that his average had usually exceeded that figure – he would by now have enjoyed, and delighted, at least half of the widows, divorcees and spinsters still residing in Birchgrove. He could only count it in his own favour that most of them remained friendly towards him.

Marigold Hicks, now. When he first became aware of her she had already been past the first flush of youth but taking great care to preserve her figure and her skin by a well-chosen diet, the avoidance of direct sunlight, regular exercise and all the unguents recommended by the magazines. Only in a really harsh light was the passing of the years detectable, and harsh lights are not usually present in rooms where a passionate woman is most appreciated. Somehow true romance had passed her by and it may be that she was becoming desperate. She was working as receptionist and nurse in the local veterinary branch practice.

Luke's Labrador at that time had been ageing and he had called in for a large bag of prescription kennel meal and some medications. Presented with the bill, he exclaimed, 'Good God! I'd be cheaper keeping a mistress.'

The lady – Marigold Jenkins, she was then – had accorded the joke rather more laughter than it was worth. 'At least the mistress would be on the National Health,' she said.

'But could she walk to heel?' he responded.

'*I* certainly could,' she said. She was looking him firmly in the eye except when she managed a quite deliberate flutter of her eyelashes. 'Let me help you out to your car with these bags and I'll show you.'

To another man, that might have been that, a laugh shared and soon forgotten; but with Luke the result had been inevitable – dinner that evening and bed that night. She had, however, been unusually insistent on care and discretion. The dinner that evening and the few that followed were taken in good but lesser known hostelries well away from Newton Lauder. The reason was soon brought to his attention. Her employer, Mr Hicks, had at last begun paying her attention; but he was a shy man, slow to make his move, and while she waited uncertainly for him to come to the point she intended to enjoy secretly such manna as might fall her way.

Eventually Mr Hicks had plucked up his courage and with it, she allowed Luke to understand, her skirt. She had exchanged beds and accepted a staid marriage in lieu of wild romance. But Mr Hicks knew which side his bread was buttered. She remained the guardian of the front desk, but ever afterwards Luke became a favoured customer – provided only that Mr Hicks was not within earshot. A woman's manner to a man with whom she has made love is seldom neutral. She may try and even succeed in hiding her past from those who come after, but there is often softness in her voice and gentleness in her movement to betray her. Or she may recall him with distaste and meet him with sharp eyes and closed posture. Marigold tried never to be seen with Luke while her husband was present.

It had been several years since he had set eyes on her, and then only from a distance. The mention of his name seemed to have brought her post-haste. The auburn of her hair now owed more to the chemist than to nature and she spent a disproportionate amount of the locals' veterinary expenditure on beauty treatments, but she was still managing to repel the old enemy, time, with dignity. Her clothes were well chosen, following the middle line between too young and too old, but she still swayed as she walked. Mary and Joline had tactfully withdrawn.

Marigold took a seat, lowering herself carefully and tucking her skirt under her knees. She allowed a momentary glow to escape and then said, 'I was sorry to hear about Emily. How is she?'

Luke gave her a version of his standard, unsatisfactory reply. 'I've been landed with custody of her children,' he went on. 'I'm trying to pick up the pieces while finding out what happened. There may be bits of information or even property scattered all over the area.' Marigold seemed about to speak but then sat back. He thought that she might be hesitating before betraying a fellow-woman's secrets to her daughters' ancestor. 'I'm told that she may have had a boyfriend,' he said. 'Can you tell me who that might be?'

She accepted his explanation at face value but still she shook her head. 'I'm afraid not. I'd tell you if I knew, but I don't. If you only want to break the news to him, I expect he knows. Bad news travels quickly around here.'

'I think you told Joline that there was a boyfriend,' Luke said gently. She nodded. 'How could you know that without knowing who?'

'Julie Benton told me. We were having coffee in the hotel – not the big one in the Square, the one up beyond the main road – and Emily walked in. When she saw us she turned around and walked out again, which set us thinking and talking. I mean, she looked quite furtive and yet she was a guest in the hotel. Julie said that perhaps she'd come to meet her lover. She knew that there was a lover because she'd been walking her niece's bearded collie near the reservoir during the dry spell that we had in May and ... you know the small wood where young couples go when they want to keep things secret?'

Luke said that he knew it. He had known it for years. In fact, he rather thought that he had taken Marigold there on a warm summer evening in ... Good God! Could it really be so long ago?

'A couple came out and walked the other way. They were too far off for her to make out who they were, but the male figure got into a car, after exchanging what could have been a kiss, and he drove off. The female figure turned back towards another car and when they got nearer to each other she saw that it was Emily, looking a little dishevelled but pretending that she had been gathering wildflowers or something.'

Parking the cars a long way apart sounded typically secretive. 'Did Julie see what colour or model the man's car was?'

'If she did, she didn't tell me.'

'She lives next door to you, doesn't she, on the far side?'

'That's right. But I don't think that they're at home just now. When the Bentons go off for a holiday it's usually to somewhere warm and her sister comes to look after the house – she only has a flat in Morningside and loves to get out into the country. I saw her there this morning, so they're probably away now. She never comes to stay while they're there – there just isn't the room because he uses the second bedroom for some hobby or other.'

Luke began to feel that he was wading in treacle. 'But you think Julie Benton knows who he is?'

'Oh, I'm sure of it. I don't remember her exact words and I don't know how she knew, but she said something about him having to be careful because of his job.'

'What job?'

'My dear, I don't know. I'm only telling you what she said; I don't know what she *meant*. Is it really so important?'

'It could be,' Luke said. 'Yes, I think it could be.'

'They don't go away for very long. Surely it can wait a couple of weeks?'

'If Emily dies,' Luke said, 'it may become urgent. It will be murder.'

The word *murder* still has its own power to shock. Marigold's mouth formed an O of surprise. Then she said, 'Oh my God! I never thought of it that way. But I still can't help you any more than that.'

Eleven

Luke's appetite had become less as his age grew more, but he was still capable of hunger and now his stomach was telling him that lunch was, if anything, slightly overdue. Mary and Joline were pressing in their invitation to stay for a snack but Luke had too much on his mind. He limped round to Helena's house. He interrupted a brisk game of rounders but was greeted affectionately by one adult, two juniors and a dog. The humans enquired anxiously about his damaged leg and then forgot about it. Helena's garden, he noticed, was looking tidier that usual. He admired one or two innovations but her grass had been marked by rough games. He accepted soup (despite the heat of the day) followed by fruit and a biscuit and cheese.

While he ate at the kitchen table, the girls resumed their play out of doors. It gave him his chance for a quiet word with Helena. 'I've begun to hear a tale,' he said. 'It's suggested that Emily had – has – a lover. Can you tell me anything?'

Helena thought for as long as it took for him to finish his soup. He thought that she might be wondering whether to tell tales or to fall back on the female conspiracy of loyal secrecy. Eventually she said, 'I've heard whispers. Nothing definite and I couldn't even tell you where I heard them. They weren't even statements, just little jokes. You know the kind of thing I mean? Somebody mentions that such-and-such a B and B isn't fussy who rents a room and doesn't even mind renting it just for an afternoon, and somebody else says that they wonder if Emily Highsmith and Whatshisname knew about it. That sort of thing.'

'And you can't even tell me who could put a real name to Whatshisname?'

'I'm afraid not. And I have a dentist's appointment this afternoon. I was going to leave the girls here with Violet in charge, but since you're here you'd better take them home. I can give you a lift.'

'Thanks,' he said. 'Rural life is hell without transport. I must phone Ledbetter and hurry him up. Mary wants me to speak to him for her anyway.'

'I'm surprised,' Helena said, 'that you don't make use of Emily's Land Rover. Why don't you?'

Luke made a face and tapped his forehead. 'Because I'm an idiot and I never thought of it, that's why. And Emily's Land Rover has manual gears, which I may not be able to manage with a sprained ankle. My new one's automatic – left foot not required.' Luke dug into his pocket. In addition to the door keys on the bunch that the social worker had passed to him and that was dragging his pocket down, there was a car key and another that looked as if it belonged to a garage door. 'The police won't have bothered with it. She had already left the car behind when she was hit. Can you keep the girls for another twenty minutes or so?'

'No problem. I have an hour in hand. We're getting on great. They're living dolls.'

'Try not to teach them Americanisms.' He smiled to soften the admonition.

'According to Bill Bryson, a lot of Americanisms are Tudor English that died out here but survived over there. Did you know that?'

Luke shook his head, unwilling to commit himself. 'I doubt if any Tudor ever said "living dolls".'

She laughed at him. 'They could have done. Just because it isn't quoted in Shakespeare...'

He hobbled round to the garage court. A day or two on third party only insurance, he decided, would hardly matter. One of the keys had a number stamped on it and it fitted the door of a lock-up with that number on a little brass plate, just about where he remembered Emily storing her Land Rover. A familiar Land Rover was waiting inside and the other key fitted it. Without starting the engine he experimented. Depressing the clutch seemed at first to be too much to ask of his damaged ankle but he found that he could operate the clutch with his heel with only slight and occasional agony. He backed out after stalling only once, got out for an uncomfortable moment to close and lock the garage and drove back to Helena's house.

A look at the rear seats revealed a neat bundle of a pillow and two rugs. That might suggest no more than a picnic. On the other hand, to the suspicious it might suggest a whole lot more. Emily had never struck him as a picnic sort of person. Before going inside to collect his great-granddaughters, he walked all round the car twice. Like any rural Land Rover, it had collected its share of marks and scratches but none of them had any meaning for him. The car seemed to be in good condition and carefully kept. He could cancel his purchase of the Terios and, if Emily's gloomy view of her own prognosis proved justified, keep her vehicle; but it seemed to be the government's intention to tax the larger four-by-fours out of existence and he had chosen the Terios with that in mind.

He gathered up Pepper and the two girls and they transferred themselves back to Whinmount. The girls seemed vastly amused by the clumsiness of his driving. He noticed, via the driving mirror, that they seemed puzzled by the pillow and rugs. 'Are those not usually in your mum's car?' he asked.

'I've seen them on a chair in Mum's bedroom,' Violet said.

'Very strange,' he said lightly and started talking about something else.

He parked in his usual place at the gable

of his house. Really, if he was getting a more respectable car he must get around to having a garage built. Indoors, he called both girls into the sitting room. They fussed over him until he was comfortable, with his foot up on a stool.

Enough time had passed, he decided, that they would not connect the rugs in the car with his next questions. 'I'm trying to look after all your mum's doings,' he said carefully, 'and that includes telling everybody who should be told. I've heard that she has a special man-friend. What can you tell me about him?'

The girls showed surprise that he was sure was genuine. 'She never brought anybody like that home,' Jane said. 'Only sometimes somebody who was married to one of her friends came along too.'

Luke smiled his thanks although it took an effort. 'Thank you, Jane. I don't suppose Pepper's had her afternoon walk yet. Why don't you take her out while Violet and I have a serious talk.'

That wording was calculated to send Jane outside without argument and it worked. Jane got to her feet. 'Are you going to phone up about Mum again?' she asked.

'In a while. I'll tell you as soon as I know anything.'

Jane nodded and made her escape. Serious talks were very much not her scene.

'Now,' Luke said, 'tell me anything you can about this elusive boyfriend.'

Violet looked worried. 'I don't know what to say. How would I know? She wouldn't bring anybody home that she wanted to be secretive about.' She paused, her brow creased with thought. 'I don't know anything much and I don't know what you want to know. It might give me a start if you went ahead and asked me questions.'

Luke was struck, not for the first time, by the logical development of her young mind. 'That's very sensible,' he said. 'Let's start with this. Did your mother often go out in the evenings, leaving you in charge? Or bringing in a sitter?'

'Leaving me in charge, for ages now.' Violet frowned at the ceiling. 'About once every week or two. She'd tell me to go to bed at my usual time, and usually she came home not long after that. I wasn't always asleep when she came in again. She always looked in on us and I could smell something fruity on her. I suppose that would be wine?'

'Probably. She wasn't out long enough to have – oh! – gone to the theatre in Edinburgh for instance?'

'Nothing like it, not for months. That did happen about last Christmas. Usually she was gone for about long enough to have watched a DVD on the telly.'

'An hour or two. I see. Did she seem her usual self when she came back?'

Violet had to think for a while. Luke kept his mental fingers crossed. Had he sailed too near the wind? But apparently not. 'She seemed to be in a good mood. Sort of contented,' Violet said.

Not much doubt, then, about what had been going on. She had been away for long enough to permit some serious dalliance, but the previous Christmas she had managed a longer absence. That could have been due to the exigencies of the man's job, but in Luke's view it was more probably due to the existence of a wife who had gone visiting at Christmas. 'Had she been out of doors?'

Violet's eyebrows, fairer than her hair, went up. 'I don't know what you mean. She couldn't get as far as the car without—'

Luke had to remind himself that he was dealing with innocent young minds. 'I didn't just mean between the house and the car. I mean as if she'd been for a country walk. Did you ever see bits of grass or dead leaves on her clothes, anything like that?'

'Mum didn't go in much for country walks,' Violet said. 'Sometimes there was dust or bitties of leaf in the clothes-brush in the hall, but I thought they came off Jane.'

'Perhaps they did.' That was about as far as he dared to push that line of questioning. Violet was remarkably innocent for her age but she must surely be aware of the significance of rustic debris on the clothes. 'When she went out in an evening like that, did she dress up specially?'

'Yes. Not evening dress specially, just sort of tea-with-Dad's-relatives specially. She'd never say why.'

I bet, Luke thought. He said, 'When people dress up for the evening, they make themselves clean and pretty, right down to the skin. They usually start by having a scented bath and end up smelling beautiful.'

Violet was nodding. 'She did that.'

'Starting with that very expensive underwear that you wanted to claim?'

'Yes. Why do people do that? I'd have thought that any old undies would be good enough if you're going out. I mean, no-body's going to see them.'

Luke was tiptoeing on thin ice. He had no intention of explaining the significance of silk underwear to his own great-grand-daughter until he had laid a foundation ... and definitely not the birds and the bees, neither of which procreated in a manner resembling the human. Once again, they were straying too close to revelations about Violet's mother. He decided that he had gone as far as he was going to go for the moment. 'Is everything tidy upstairs?' he asked.

'Yes. Definitely.'

'Promise?'

'I promise.'

'You run along then and see if you can catch up with Jane. When you come back I may have some news for you.'

Violet looked doubtful at being banished but she suddenly capitulated and left by the French windows. With some difficulty, Luke pushed himself to his feet, picked up his stick and limped out as far as the Land Rover. The glove compartment was, as he expected, locked but the ignition key un-locked it. Luke was not unfamiliar with womanly things. He was left in no doubt that his granddaughter-in-law had not intended to remain celibate, nor to become pregnant again. There were dead leaves and pine needles in the rug on the back seat. His doubts were disappearing, one by one. He would have to deliver the rugs to DI Fellowes for forensic study. There would probably be DNA traces that would provide clinching proof later. He just hoped, for the girls' sake, that none of this would ever have to come out in court.

He returned inside and headed for his workroom. Using his mobile phone, he called the hospital. Emily was scheduled for more surgery later that day. For the moment, she was still holding her own. He asked to be put in touch with whoever had undressed her on admission. Eventually he found himself speaking to a Nurse Weimms. She had, she said, been wondering who to speak to. It was all in a terrible mess, she said, but some of it had been very expensive. The blood might wash out but some of the other damage would be difficult to repair. A glance through Helena's cupboards had assured Luke that there need be no shortage of delicate fripperies if Emily recovered or whenever the girls were old enough for that sort of thing. 'Burn it,' he said, 'or give it to a passing tramp.'

His next call was to Julie Benton's house. Her sister came to the phone. 'It's very urgent that I speak with Julie,' he said. 'Can you give me a number to ring?'

The sister made a noise that is usually transcribed as Humph! 'I hae a number but you'll hae hell's own job calling it, a lot of foreigners on the other end who don't understand English and don't want to let you speak to aabody.' (Luke had forgotten Julie's execrable Glasgow accent until he heard it echoed again in her sister's voice.) 'But she calls home every evening, to be sure that everything's all right. If you could be here before eight, you could maybe speak to her.'

'How long is she away for?'

'They have another three weeks.'

That could be too long. 'I'll be with you just before eight.'

To be sure that he was not wasting his time, Luke phoned Detective Inspector Fellowes. But Inspector Fellowes had not received more than the vaguest hints that the injured lady might have had a lover and while prepared to believe that such could be the case nothing that had occurred so far had given him the faintest idea who it could be. He would collect the rugs from the Land Rover and if Luke could help towards discovering the identity of the mystery lover he would earn undying gratitude.

So some minutes before eight, Luke hobbled from the Land Rover and presented himself at Mrs Benton's door. Her sister let him in and he was reminded of the several reasons why he had never contemplated an affair with Julie. The sister was friendly and even slightly flirtatious but, being small, pasty and rather simian in appearance, was her sibling's clone. She also had a similar metallic voice and an execrable accent.

Luke struggled to make polite conversation. It was twenty agonising minutes before the telephone made its double beep. Then there was a further lengthy delay while the two sisters exchanged news. He had never been familiar with the Glasgow accent and he had great difficulty following much of what was said but he was almost sure that neither news nor enquiries about Emily had been exchanged.

At last Julie's sister passed him the phone. But his troubles were not over. In addition to the thick accent and the excitement engendered by suddenly finding herself speaking to a comparative stranger, Mrs Benton seemed to have contracted a cold. She also had a habit of letting her voice drop just as she arrived at the crux of what she was saying. Furthermore, the line was very bad, subject to sudden interruptions in a language that he thought might be Portuguese. Try as he might, he could hardly make out the whole of a single sentence. He tried to persuade Julie's sister to do the talking and listening for him, but she had no intention of taking the responsibility. He let her end the call.

'The next time you speak to her,' he said, 'could you ask her whether there's somebody there who...' His voice trailed away. How exactly was he to word his query? *Who speaks in a voice a non-Glaswegian can understand?* That would not be the way to gain maximum help and cooperation. 'Where was she speaking from?' he asked.

'Madeira.'

That was quite different.

Many years earlier, when Luke was not long embarked on his chosen career, Sr Bustini had already been on the way to becoming a power in the world of hotels and leisure resorts. He had been in the process of purchasing a large but rundown country hotel in the Borders when he discovered that his daughter was pregnant by his male secretary. Portuguese pride demanded urgent action; Scots law forbade the first action that came to mind.

Conveniently, both the participants were travelling with him at the time so that, even in Scotland, it was easy to arrange a hasty marriage. Luke had previously furnished the photographs of another hotel for the brochures so Sr Bustini had engaged him to take a few shots of an occasion of which he thought he might prefer not to be reminded. Paying maximum attention to lighting and camera angles, Luke had managed to make the bride (who, despite the advantages of bridal costume looked undeniably plain if not verging on ugly) appear pretty and almost beautiful. He had gone on to photograph the refurbished hotel for a brochure and had contrived to present the building, which though internally charming was externally Scottish and very dour, as appearing welcoming and quite jolly in places. As a result, Luke had flown around the world many times as the Bustini empire grew, taking publicity, brochure and poster shots of ever larger and more prestigious projects. The daughter's marriage had turned out to be more successful than most and the new son-in-law was not only clever but also honest. Sr Bustini had passed away but his empire was now mainly in the daughter's hands and managed by her husband, who still felt indebted to Luke for easing his acceptance into the family.

An offer of the commission to photograph the newest hotel on Madeira had been in his emails when he got around to opening them the previous day. He had been on the point of turning it down, partly because of his new responsibilities but also because on Madeira (where very few foodstuffs except fruit can be locally produced) the scenery, climate and company might be all that a man could desire but he had found the cuisine usually inferior to the best that Scotland can provide. The coincidence, however, presented an opportunity to do exactly what he wanted to do at somebody else's expense and to be handsomely paid for it. This was too good to ignore.

So next morning, Luke found himself leaving his great-granddaughters with Helena and, later, Emily's Land Rover in the secure parking at Glasgow Airport. He had managed to achieve, with his pain-killers, the delicate balance between anaesthesia and intoxication. He had also remembered an almost forgotten knack of clutchless gear changing. Use of his left foot and damaged ankle was only necessary when he was forced to come to a complete halt and such occasions could be minimized by use of the extra-low bottom gear. He managed the trip without doing irreparable damage to the transmission or to his ankle. He limped, hobbled and hopped to the check-in, thankful to be relieved of his small case and his camera-bag.

He surrendered himself to the endless delays of Security and then the comfortless squalor provided by Messrs Boeing. Not being a midget, his choices of sitting position were limited, ranging between the uncomfortable and the insupportable. As they flew, he mused. The car market had passed largely into Japanese hands and the Japs were a small people, but they studied their market and so it was rare for their cars to be seriously undersized. Americans were, on average, large. Luke withdrew his legs from the aisle to let the trolley go by and then eased his bottom into a new but just as painful position. So how was it that their planes offered comfort only to little people? The answer, he supposed, was that they built their planes to specifications provided by the operators, and these people too were small ... in mind and body, too small-minded to allow for the comfort of travellers if another few seats could possibly be squeezed in.

With such uncharitable thoughts the four hours of misery were passed, until at last he saw the steep hillside close to Funchal Airport rising beside the wing. The plane, caught in the eternal turbulence, touched down with a thump that made his teeth snap together.

Either the late Sr Bustini's daughter or his son-in-law retained grateful memories because a limousine with darkened windows had been sent to collect him, driven by a chauffeur who refused to let him carry a single item of his own luggage. Not for him the crowded coach from the airport near Santa Catarina. The chauffeur found Luke a seat in the airport, disappeared for a few minutes and returned with a wheelchair. Luke was conveyed to the limousine and wafted along the clifftop motorway, around the back of Funchal and down to the new hotel. This was already in occupation, mostly by VIP guests, in preparation for the opening festivities. Special efforts had been made with the landscaping; and money had been spent on importing plants already mature. The hotel, he thought, had been sited with a view to preserving many of the original palm trees.

He was allotted a room on the first floor with a balcony overlooking the gardens, the swimming pools and over the Bay of Funchal to the Atlantic and the three 'Desertas' islands on the horizon. The light was already softening from the sometimes harsh glare of full day. He hobbled outside with his camera bag. He knew exactly what was wanted. Flower photographs were already in overprovision on the 'Island of Flowers'. The management needed photographs of the hotel, using flowers or any other resource to convey an impression of welcoming, easygoing luxury, fun and frolic. This was no problem – he had performed the same magic a thousand times before. What the grey concrete buildings lacked in sympathetic materials they made up with ingenious curvilinear engineering forms reflected in the landscaping.

Even the freeloading celebs obliged, by moving as needed and smiling when told. A gardener was appointed to follow him around and, where required, to cut a branch of blossom to dangle over him as if he were photographing from below a tree; or to lift a plant to where he could get his shot over or through it. The hotel even provided another wheelchair, to be pushed by the same gardener.

When the light was too far gone, he went in to dinner. Nothing had changed very much since his last visit. Meat tends to be tough when it has to be purchased over the phone and shipped or flown out. Madeira is a volcanic mountain peak jutting out of deep ocean. Swordfish and tuna could be caught but the smaller fish, while acceptable, have been imported and may not be perfectly fresh. Fruit is excellent. Vegetable soup, fish pie and fruit salad made an excellent meal with a glass or two of Madeiran wine. He spent the evening working on his interior shots. The hotel was full of female talent, much of which he had seen earlier, bathing topless among the flowers. Years ago he might have been tempted into pursuit, but he was past that sort of thing, he told himself. He went to bed early.

At breakfast, he found himself sharing his table with a Dutchman who identified the single bloom that decorated each table as a protea. He was intrigued to see Luke beginning breakfast by mixing orange juice with wine provided by the management. 'In Britain,' Luke explained, 'we call it a "Bucks Fizz". But it should be made with real, proper Champagne, not with sparkling Portuguese. I suppose that makes it a Cadiz Fizz.'

'Cadiz,' said the Dutchman, 'would be Spain, not Portugal. What you have made would be a Lisbon Fizz.'

'Lizz fizz for short?'

'But of course.'

Luke had no intention of wrestling verbally with foreign telephone exchanges. He induced the receptionist to take on the duty. That young lady, while mildly indignant at being asked to contact a different and therefore inferior hotel, managed to place the call only to find that the lady Luke was seeking had gone on a tour to the Botanic Garden. She would return for lunch.

He shook his head. The sun would not even shine on the Botanic Garden until afternoon. He had been nursing a faint hope that he could interview Mrs Benton in the morning and get an afternoon plane home, but that was out of the window. However, cloud had come over the sun. The black cloud that often hangs above the mountain had returned. The diffused light made possible certain other views, less cluttered with hotel guests, most of who remained indoors. He made a quick phone call home and then went out. A breeze attracted three hang-glider pilots who had found an updraught close to the shore and were swooping overhead. (Later he picked his best shot of the hotel with guests laughing and looking up. He removed the black cloud, substituted an area of hillside and printed in the hang-gliders. The result showed the hotel as the place for sport and frolic. It became the hotel's poster.)

After a snack lunch beside one of the pools, he commandeered the limo again and was driven higher up the hillside to the hotel that the Bentons had chosen. They had finished lunch but joined him for coffee on a terrace boasting an even more spectacular view.

He had decided to make no mention of malicious intent, although if rumours were circulating at home they would no doubt reach them here. 'You may have heard,' he said, 'that Emily Highsmith, my grand-daughter-in-law, was seriously injured last Friday. She's having surgery but there's no certainty that she'll survive. I've been land-ed with the task of looking after the girls and attending to her affairs. I've been hearing about a man-friend but nobody can tell me who he is. I must track him down. I want to find out whether there have been any gifts or loans, in either direction, or any kind of obligations. I'm told that you saw them together once.'

'Aye. Mebbe. But they was a long way aff.' (Luke's spirits fell. Had he come all this way for nothing? Except, of course, for a highly desirable fee. Against which was having to listen to a voice that could have humbled a circular saw.) 'I seed him again, though.'

'You did?' Luke's spirits took a sudden

turn for the better

'Aye. Leastways I saw his car. I'd walked past it the time before. It was a green Sierra with a plate that spelled out my name, Julie B, give or take a bit. Then Donnie here took me up to the Glenamis Hotel on the road to Peebles, and I seen the same car and a man getting out of it who looked awful like the mannie I seen with Mrs Highsmith. A big, sonsie man with a bushy black moustache, in a Glengarry bonnet. I think he owns the place.'

The insignificant Donnie spoke up for the first time. In a deep, rumbling voice that seemed totally inappropriate to his small frame he said, 'He's the manager.'

Luke managed to convey his thanks and farewells without provoking Mrs Benton into further speech. He flew home the next day. By good fortune the only seats available were in first class, so that he was almost comfortable.

Twelve

Luke's luck continued to hold. Chatting to his neighbour on the plane, he found that the younger man was on his way home to Bathgate and intended to phone a friend to come and collect him. He claimed to be familiar with Land Rovers. In case the man was exaggerating his own abilities in order to save on transport, Luke slipped in a technical question about the transfer box, which was answered in greater depth than Luke could wholly understand. So Luke found himself being chauffeured all the way to Newton Lauder where his own car, complete with automatic gearbox, was now awaiting him. Thus he could honour their agreement and drive his new friend back round the Edinburgh Ring Road and homeward, using the automatic gears and not needing the use of his still throbbing left ankle at all. He left Emily's Land Rover and its keys with young Ledbetter, to deliver to her lock-up pending a decision about selling it.

He should, he now realized, have bargained harder with young Ledbetter and made him throw in a hands-free phone kit, for lack of which he had to pull into a lay-by. His great-granddaughters, as he expected, were still at Menu, Helena's house. The hour by now being late he asked Helena to keep them for another night. His next call informed him that DI Fellowes was off duty and not at home. He left a message inviting the DI to call on him next morning. The nursing staff at the New Royal assured him that Emily had survived another serious operation and was holding her own.

The fine weather had given way to drizzle and a cold breeze, both of which came as a shock after Madeira. He reached home and parked the Terios where his Land Rover used to stand. The house still held the warmth and scents of his great-granddaughters, which made this more of a homecoming than his more usual returns to a cold and empty house. He made a snack to supplement the inadequate aircraft meal and took himself to his bed.

As usual, he left his new phone beside the bed, on charge but switched on; otherwise he would have missed the call that woke him out of a deep, tired sleep at around his usual time for wakening. The call was from the New Royal. Emily's doctor, sounding suitably grave, informed him that the patient had suffered a serious stroke during the night. She would certainly not be fit to undergo further surgery for some time. It was too early to say how she would progress and what damage would have been done to her faculties. For the moment, she would not know Mr Grant. Visitors were not being encouraged even if he made the trip.

Luke would have been pleased to go back to sleep but the news had jerked him awake. Major changes to several lives were in the air. He pondered while he ate breakfast and by the time Helena arrived bringing the two girls and Pepper he had decided once again that truth was the best policy. Any evasions, when detected, would suggest a greater and more imminent tragedy than the real facts and would damage their trust in him for the future. He led them into the sitting room and made sure that he shared the couch with Jane.

'Something's wrong, isn't it?' Violet said. 'Is it Mum?'

'She had a setback during the night,' said Luke. It seemed to be the way to begin breaking the bad news, springing off from an assurance that their mother was still alive. 'She was having another operation and it didn't go the way it was planned. She had a stroke.'

Jane turned very white. He put an arm around her. 'What's a stroke?' she asked.

Luke realized that he was unsure of the medical details. 'I think it means a clot of blood reaching the brain and damaging it. People can recover completely from a stroke. Sometimes you wouldn't even know that they'd had a stroke at all. But this seems to have been a serious one. They won't be able to give her any more operations for now. We may eventually have to bring her here and nurse her for a long time.'

There was silence so complete that Luke could hear the breeze stirring in the trees outside and a tractor working in a distant field. 'That's awful,' Helena breathed.

At last Luke heard and felt Jane sigh. Pepper moved to her side and laid a paw on her knee. 'Poor Mum,' Jane said.

'Yes,' said Luke. He searched in vain for more words of comfort. 'Has Pepper been walked?' he asked.

Helena leaped to his aid. She stood up and moved to the French windows. 'We'll take her out. Your great-granddad will have a lot to do.' Luke gave her a smile.

'I'll stay,' Violet said. 'You two go.'

'All right,' Jane said. 'Come on, Poopumninc.' Pepper followed obediently.

Luke and Violet had the room to themselves. '*What* did she call Pepper?'

'Poopumninc.' Violet brightened for a moment. 'It's what Mrs Harper called her once, when Pepper was being a bit daft. It means a backward sort of nincompoop.'

'She seems like that sometimes,' Luke said. 'All Labradors do. But only sometimes.'

'Sometimes she farts,' said Violet. 'Mrs Harper called her Flatulent Flora. And she sang "Come to me, my coprophagic baby." GG, what does coprophagic mean?'

Luke had been charmed by Helena's sense of humour but had never realized that she was hiding quite such a ribald streak. The revelation he found slightly pleasing but this was hardly the moment for enquiring into it and Luke did not feel up to what would undoubtedly become a lengthy discussion of the nature, causes and treatment of coprophagia. 'Nothing that you should be thinking about at your age. Did you want anything special or just a shoulder to cry on? That's just an expression,' he added quickly in case Violet should take him literally.

She lifted her child-sized nose. It was a sign of her youth that she could go from laughter to tears in an instant. 'I do know that, GG,' she said. 'I wanted to ask you something. It doesn't look good for Mum, does it?'

'People do make the most remarkable recoveries. And, of course, she's in one of the best places to make the most of her chances. Development in medical science...'

Violet frowned and made a dismissive gesture. 'Be honest, GG. Wouldn't you say that she has a small chance of making it, and if she does make it she'll have even less chance of ever being able to do things for herself? Whatever you tell me,' she added, I won't pass it on to Jane unless she asks me a direct question. Always the truth, remember?'

Luke was beginning to wish that he had

not been quite so insistent on eternal honesty. Scope for an occasional white lie would have been welcome, but it was important to retain their trust. 'I simply don't know enough to comment,' he said. 'On the basis of what little I know so far, it does look that way. But I could be quite wrong. I told you, I've met people who'd had strokes and you'd never know it, and to have had it in a major hospital must increase her chances.'

'So it's not good.' Violet got up and crossed to the settee. She sat down beside her great-grandfather and hugged his upper arm. 'GG, I'm unhappy—'

'Of course—'

She shook his arm and then buried her face behind it. Her voice was muffled. 'GG, I'm unhappy because I'm not unhappy. Do you understand?'

Luke found that he could make a sort of offbeat sense out of it. 'I believe I do. I'll understand better if you explain.'

She took a deep breath. 'My mother is desperately ill,' she said. 'That is a fact. I should be crying my eyes out but I'm not. It's not that I actively dislike her. I can view her quite dispassionately – is that the right word? – and make a comparison with other mums. It's more that I don't positively like her when I should. Perhaps I'm a little afraid of her. I certainly don't think I love her, the way I'm supposed to. She's done her best for us, always, but does it as a duty, a rather annoying duty, not out of love. She's never close. There's always coldness like a barrier. I ... I'm trying not to accept the fact that a part of me doesn't wish her any harm but does wish that we could go on living here always with you and Mrs Harper. We've never been so happy. Does that make me a bad person?'

He put his arm round her as he had for Jane. 'No. The fact that you worry about it is proof enough. These conflicts, pulling you two ways at once, happen often enough in life. Being able to see both sides of an argument lays you open to all kinds of doubts. The better person you are, the more liable you'll be to worry about them when a more selfish, thoughtless person would shrug them off and think, "I'm all right, Jack." Now just clear your mind and concentrate on doing your best from day to day. Don't let abstract thoughts get to you.'

Violet nodded. She pushed herself upright, pulled the clean handkerchief out of the breast pocket of his old blazer and blew her nose roughly. 'GG, are you going to marry Mrs Harper?'

'The question hasn't arisen,' he said.

'But will it? You get on very well.'

'True. But we wrinklies don't often marry. We're past the age when children would be likely to come along.' He decided to skip past the question of nasty diseases. 'Marriage is mostly to ensure that the family is looked after but it can bring all sorts of complications about inheritance. I would want to leave you my possessions, you and Jane between you, without worrying about somebody else's relatives turning up and saying "Hoy! This was always supposed to come to me." You see what I mean?'

'So there's no reason why you and Mrs Harper shouldn't move in together?' Violet was looking at him very earnestly. 'And don't call yourself a wrinkly. Mr Calder has more wrinkles than you do.'

'Why this sudden onrush of matchmaking?' Luke asked. 'Trying to marry off your great-grandfather! I never heard of such a thing. Is it just feminine sentimentality or what?'

'I'll tell you,' Violet said. She then sat in

silence for a full minute. 'What it is,' she said at last, 'is that Jane and I were talking about what we'd really like to happen if things had to change. And change does seem to be happening whether we want it to or not. We wondered what would be the best sort of life for us. And we thought that living with you and Mrs Harper – she asked us to call her Helena but that seems sort of cheeky – might make us into a sort of family. And what you said about older people not marrying makes it easier, because if Mum does make it but needs nursing we could bring her here and look after her together.'

Luke found himself completely lost for words. There was a ring at the doorbell and Violet went to let the visitor in. It was one of the few occasions in his life that Luke was pleased by the arrival of the police.

The fine weather had made a tentative return. In its honour Detective Inspector Fellowes had dispensed with his jacket and was wearing his shirt open at the neck. The lack of formality suited his boyish build, taking years away from him. It also encouraged Luke to think about fresh air and sunshine. He persuaded Violet to set out two folding chairs on the small terrace and then to set off to overtake the walkers.

When the two men were settled, each with a mug of coffee, Luke said, 'I have two pieces of information for you. I went all the way to Madeira to secure the first fragment. Don't look so panicked,' he added quickly. 'I wasn't thinking of asking you to pay my expenses.'

'You'd have been out of luck if you had.'

'That's what I thought. I won't pretend that I went all that way just to save you from having to put your questions through the Madeiran police or by phone. And, frankly, such was the accent of my informant I doubt if anyone but a born Glaswegian could have made sense of it. I had the chance to earn a little of my living along the way.

'Emily's lover has something to do with the Glenamis Hotel, possibly as manager. In case there's any dubiety, he's said to be a sonsie man with a bushy black moustache and his car is a green Sierra with registration letters that seem to spell out Julie B. You can ask Mrs Benton about it when she returns from Madeira.'

'That's helpful,' Fellowes acknowledged.

'But you yourself pointed out the difficulty that a stranger would have in lying in wait in the garage court. And it does seem that she had expected to meet him.'

'She was dressed for meeting a lover,' Luke said. 'Right down to the skin.'

'Well, yes.' Luke thought that for two pins the Inspector would have produced a nudge and a wink. 'I didn't know whether you knew that. I wasn't exactly trying to spare your blushes by omitting that detail; I was hoping to leave your illusions intact, if you still had any. She is, after all, your relative by marriage. From the medical report it seems that she had not yet had sex, but they were far more concerned with her medical condition than with forensic evidence. We can certainly assume that she had expectations of that nature. Whether or not the gentleman from the Glenamis Hotel had been the object of her expectations, he must know the answers to a dozen background questions that we want answered. What was the other news?'

'The other news is not good. Emily had a bad stroke last night during surgery. They don't expect to have her fit for more surgery, which she needs, for some time to come. Unspoken were the words *if at all.* I don't know any more than that; I can only say that it doesn't sound very hopeful. I think it's very unlikely that she'll ever be able to make a statement. If she dies now, that would make it a case of murder?'

The DI was looking very serious. 'Assuming that the damage was deliberate, if she dies within a year and a day it counts as murder.'

'You'll be taking it more seriously?'

The DI drew himself up, as much as one can draw oneself up in a low, garden chair. 'We are already taking it seriously, I can assure you. My small team is busily tying up the loose ends of its earlier cases. By tomorrow, I hope to turn this into a properly conducted investigation instead of a rather haphazard enquiry. Meantime, I have already followed up much of what you've given me.' The DI's dark flush showed up against his pale, freckled skin, exaggerating his youthful look and causing Luke to forget, for moments at a time, that the other was a policeman. 'I called on Miss Henderson and Mrs Kemp. You wouldn't believe ... But their alibis stand up.'

'They revenged themselves on you, did

they?' Luke asked.

'I'm not here to answer questions,' the inspector said stiffly.

Luke had been tempted to enjoy a little needling. The picture of the staid and married detective inspector being invited to wrestle with a nearly nude Joline Henderson was compelling but he decided to let the opportunity slip by. He could coax the whole story out of the two ladies later. 'Perhaps you could answer this one. You said that you gave my ... Emily ... a warning about rumourmongering and you said that the anonymous letters then stopped. But did you ever find out who wrote them? And was it Emily?'

'That,' said the inspector, 'is two questions. The answer to the first is "Yes". I must not answer the second. There was no proof but the matter is closed. To get back to the subject under discussion, I'm working my way through the other locals who were not at the darts match nor the bridge tournament but so far most of them seem to have been in the presence of the town's most trustworthy citizens.'

'What do you do now? Widen the net?'

'That, and go back over earlier statements,

looking at what may have been missed, for contradictions and lies. You, for instance. Tell me again how you got on with your granddaughter-in-law.'

Luke felt a sudden pain in his chest. He put a hand to his pocket but felt an immediate grasp of his wrist by a strong hand. 'What do you want from your pocket?' the DI asked sternly. There could be no doubt that he was a policeman again.

Luke took his hand out slowly. He could feel sweat on his forehead. 'I am not planning to take poison, if that's what you think. The nitro pills are for my heart. Do you mind? When you sprang that on me I felt a sudden pain. I still do.'

DI Fellowes looked at the label on the bottle and then into Luke's face. He released his grip and sat down again. 'My apologies,' he said. 'I have to be careful. When you're ready, please answer the question. Or, if you want to see a doctor say the word.'

Luke took one of the pills under his tongue and waited with his eyes closed. The pain began to abate. He wasn't too sure of his bowels but he decided to take a chance. After another minute or two he opened his eyes and said, 'You were asking how I got on with Emily. I thought I'd told you that.' He thought of refusing to repeat himself until his solicitor was present, but with his solicitor also acting for Emily the gesture might have caused more fuss than it settled. 'We didn't like each other,' he said, '– a fact that she reminded me of when I saw her a couple of days ago. She was a remarkably stiff-necked and opinionated woman. She refused to believe openly in political correctness but she followed its precepts all the time. She pretended to be very upright in all that she did and disapproving of everybody else. In fact, whatever somebody else enjoyed had to be wrong. But beneath it all ... she had a secret lover and she was capable of all sorts of mean little revenges, usually by revealing secrets or inventing scurrilous rumours.'

DI Fellowes had been nodding and half-smiling. Now he said, 'I hear rumours too. They say that there was a sudden coldness between you and Mrs Highsmith.'

Luke sighed. 'There had been no warmth between us for years. I thought I told you so. We disliked each other intensely.'

'But more so than usual during the past month or so?'

'Perhaps. We had a more than usually angry argument a few weeks ago. I adore my great-granddaughters and she was making it more and more difficult for me to see them. I told her that she was being hurtful to no good end; that I was surely entitled at my age to enjoy my time with my great-granddaughters and that her attitude could only be doing them harm. She replied...' Luke stopped and swallowed.

'Yes?'

'I could hardly believe that anyone could be so vicious. She said that she was keeping them safe from me or any other man with my reputation. I was too angry to trust myself. I turned and walked away.'

'And what was your relationship after that?'

'I never saw her again until after the accident when I saw her in hospital. On that occasion she seemed to have forgotten that there had ever been anything more than a mild dislike between us and I could hardly rake up with a critically damaged woman what to me had been unforgivable. Ask whoever you like, you won't find anyone truthful who says that he or she saw us together. Occasionally I'd meet Violet in the street or out walking but it was quite clear that she – probably both of them – had been told to stay away from me.'

'That must have hurt.'

'It did, and I think that it hurt them quite as much as it hurt me. Quite enough to give rise to murder if I was that sort of person, which I'm not. Just as well that my time's accounted for, isn't it? Mrs Harper left me here, drove to the garage court and found her. That surely rules me out.'

The DI looked at Luke in a manner that Luke, in retrospect, could only think of as pitying. 'If she is to be believed. And it doesn't rule out Mrs Harper,' he said. 'Her Land Rover has been tested but without finding any traces of blood. But then, she could have exchanged vehicles with you until next day. And your Land Rover then took a convenient dive into the canal.'

Luke paused to explore his own senses but his angina was not making a return. He was finding it very difficult to think logically about a scenario which he was quite sure had never happened. He seized on the one aspect that, for him, stood out clearly. As far as I know,' he said, 'Helena Harper never had a fight with Mrs Highsmith. Why on earth would she want to hurt her?'

The DI looked hard at Luke. 'Would you prefer that we continued this discussion in the presence of your doctor? Or your solicitor?'

Luke breathed deeply for a few seconds and decided that the spasm had indeed passed. He shook his head.

'Sometimes,' the DI said reflectively, 'if you wonder why somebody did something, it helps to consider what actually happened at the end of the day. In this instance, the outcome is that you have control of your great-granddaughters.'

'That might, just might, furnish a motive for me, not that I would contemplate such a thing. It would not make a motive for Helena Harper.'

'Except,' said the DI slowly, 'that Mrs Harper worships the ground you walk on, as the saying is. One has only to see her in your presence to see that she adores you. She would be totally under your influence.'

Luke opened his mouth without finding anything to say.

DI Fellowes spent most of the next hour questioning Luke about his relationship with Helena Harper and their movements on the night of Emily Highsmith's injuries. He made no secret of his intention of making similar enquiries of Helena; indeed, Luke discovered later that Helena was already being questioned by a woman detective sergeant. It was therefore just as well that he was absolutely frank about their relationship and the alternative nature of their loving. 'I don't think that Helena Harper would kill for me,' he finished. 'I certainly wouldn't have asked her to do so. And if I had put aside my prejudices and made such a request, my granddaughter-in-law would not have been the subject. I can think of several politicians and one or two muck-raking journalists who would come higher on the list.'

In answering the other questions he was somewhat *distrait*. The DI and Violet between them had given him something new to think about. When DI Fellowes moved on to the subject of the ladies who Luke had interviewed about the injuries to Emily Highsmith, Luke had difficulty recalling the details and was quite unable to read any buried secrets or spot any contradictions in what had been said.

'I might have more chance of spotting

discrepancies,' Luke said at last, irritably, 'if you told me whose alibis had stood up to examination.'

'I can't possibly do that.'

Luke had had more than enough. 'In that case, bugger off. I thought you owed me that much. If you don't agree you can approach me through my solicitor.'

The DI thought it over and then sighed. 'I can't name any names except those of your two ladyfriends, Joline Henderson and Mary Kemp. Theirs were confirmed exactly as told to you. But I'll give you some statistics. Of the six couples and ten singles unaccounted for, one couple was at the theatre in Edinburgh and two couples made up a party to go to a casino, also in Edinburgh. Two couples were together in one house,' the DI said with distaste. 'What they were doing was anybody's guess but the from-home couple didn't go home until the morning. The other couple claims to have been asleep in their own bed, and since they tot up to nearly a hundred and fifty years between them I think we can believe them.

'Of the ten singletons, we can account for six at a sweep because there was a card school in one house that they all attended.

The other four individuals – two households sharing – also shared a car to go to a dinner-dance in Dalkeith.'

While acknowledging that the DI had only been doing his job, Luke still resented the suggestion that either he or Helena, or both in collusion, had made a serious attempt on the life of his granddaughter-in-law. His only comfort was that he had obtained his revenge even before the offence had been given. Many men, he was sure, would have enjoyed featuring as the victims of that particular revenge, but not the upright DI Fellowes.

The source of his distraction was simple. It had suddenly been thrust on his attention that, if Emily had repeated her calumny in any other circles, suspicion of paedophilia might become attached to him. Unless, of course, he took Helena into his household or even married her. There would be several advantages, not all of them romantic; and her chaperonage would be an important one of them.

Thirteen

Luke was woken early by the telephone which was, as usual, on charge by his side. The voice which had been substituted for the ringing tone, of the young lady remarking in sexy tones that she was ready, still came as a surprise to him and it took him a few seconds to realize that this had neither been overnight company nor a beautiful dream. Then he had an immediate sense of doom. Medical staff work to a different rhythm from ordinary mortals. Luke could not think of anyone else of his acquaintance who greeted the dawn with a telephone in the hand.

His apprehension turned out to be justified. A dispassionate voice told him briskly but not unsympathetically that Mrs Highsmith had died an hour earlier. There would be a post-mortem examination but he should make arrangements with his preferred undertaker. Luke explained that he personally had been in an accident and would not be coming through in the immediate future. In view of the damage to her clothing, it could be disposed of. He was assured that there had been nothing of significance about her person except for a manicure set and some items of jewellery that would be sent to him by Securicor, at his expense.

After such a beginning, the day began with surprising normality; but the girls, at breakfast, soon noticed that he was not his usual self. 'I heard your phone make its noise. I thought for a moment that you had somebody with you until I remembered. It's Mum, isn't it?' Violet said. Luke thought that she was developing a talent for muscle-reading. 'Has she died?'

'I'm afraid so. I've been wondering how to break it to you, but now it's out.'

Jane looked at him, round-eyed. 'Does this mean that we'll go on living with you?'

'Yes, it does,' Luke said. 'I hope that pleases you.'

'In a way it does, but not the reason for it. And what about Aunt Helena?' said Violet.

'That is none of your damn business just yet.'

'Can I be a bridesmaid?' asked Jane.

'You are leaping far too far ahead,' Luke said sternly.

The diversion served to turn their minds partially aside from death and, though there were one or two instances of tears over incidents that would not normally have called for them, the sisters seemed to be taking it well and soon resumed normal life. They even began, quite willingly, to clean and tidy the house and make the beds while Luke went in to Newton Lauder to be advised by Mr Enterkin about finances and bequests. These were predictable and mundane. Emily's widow's pension had died with her but she left a useful capital sum in trust for her daughters.

Mr Enterkin's advice accorded with Luke's opinion – that it would be foolish to leave valuables in an unoccupied house while waiting for the legal processes to be completed. The afternoon was therefore spent transferring any of Emily's more precious items to Luke's house along with Emily's better clothes (to be put in store *sine die*) and some more of the girls' treasures. The Terios being small, quite a number of journeys were called for, but the distance was short.

Luke had found time to phone the news to Helena. She had risen to the occasion. 'You'll be busy,' she told Luke. 'Would you like to come to me for a meal?'

'You come to us,' Luke said. 'We're stacked up with food for at least three.'

'I'll come and cook. That will let you get on.'

'Bless you!'

Dusty and sweaty, Luke and the girls freshened up and the four sat down to a meal of lemon sole followed by strawberries and ice cream. Comfortably replete, Luke and Helena settled on the terrace for the afternoon, their chairs close enough for a hand-clasp. The girls had each been allocated a corner of lawn that had once been flower-bed, to dig over and grow flowers or vegetables, and they were busily engaged.

'What's wrong?' Helena asked. 'Even allowing for the loss of a granddaughter-in-law who you didn't particularly like, you're not your usual self. I could almost say that you're not *even* your usual self.'

'It's not much fun growing old,' Luke said. 'I'm wondering whether I have the stamina to live up to a pair of teenagers and see them through to maturity.'

'I'm growing old too. We all grow old. We can grow old together. I'm not as old as you are...'

'Nobody's as old as I am.' Luke sighed. 'When I was young, if I had a pain I knew that it wouldn't go on for ever. The bruise would mend, the cut would heal or my mother would give me something to make the bellyache go away. Now each time that I feel a new pain I know that it's here for keeps. I used to wonder how old people suffer their aches and pains with so little complaint and even keep smiling. Now I know that those are the ones who still believe that it will get better.'

Helena's hold on his hand tightened. 'How's your sprain?' she asked.

Luke gave a reluctant chuckle. 'All right, bad example. My sprain does get a little better every day, thanks to the stuff I have to wash off my hands before I touch anything. But I look across the valley and I see the high hills and I know that I'll never be fit to climb them again. That's what hurts, knowing that I've done things for the last time.'

'The views may be further from higher up but they're prettier lower down. I think you're depressed because we haven't had nooky for a while. That's something that you haven't done for the last time.' She was speaking softly but she lowered her voice still further. 'How about tonight? You can tie me up if you like.'

Luke looked at her. There was no coyness in her manner, just a willingness to please. He noticed for the hundredth time that along with her figure she had retained a sort of beauty. It was the beauty of an idealized mother-figure, small and slightly plump, of any age; but that did not lessen her attraction. He wondered again that her eyes, which were large, grey and luminous, managed to be moist without being watery. They were beautiful eyes, he decided. He felt a sudden desire, not so much physical as nostalgic. 'Yes,' he said. 'Are you trying to be a little mother to me?'

She gave a little laugh that, now that he had come to notice it, was noticeably immodest. She lowered her voice again until she was barely audible. 'Did your mother ever invite you for an evening of bondage nooky? I'll have to nip home and change into some pretties; I mustn't dispel your illusions. And, Luke, I think you should back away from the investigation now,'

Helena said bravely, returning to her normal tones. 'You've helped Ian Fellowes all you can. It seems that almost everybody for miles around has an alibi. The police have the resources for testing alibis but you don't. I think you should leave it to them. I don't want somebody else, or the same one, thinking that you're getting too close and having another go at you. Maybe cutting something else, like your throat.'

'I was beginning to think the same thing.'

They sat in silence, drinking in the peace and contemplating the future. The shadows were stretching out and the peace of evening was in the air. Only the crows were noisy.

Several days went by in tranquillity. Luke began to hope that the worst was past. He was not a ready mixer in local society but he had the impression that any speculation about Emily's accident was dying down. Any question of a funeral was postponed indefinitely, the unfortunate Emily being preserved in a chilled state pending a decision by the procurator fiscal as to the cause of death, or by a sheriff and jury if the fiscal so decided. Luke turned his mind away from wondering whether anyone who had seemed so cold in life would care about a little frost after death, but the thought persisted in spite of him.

Luke's ankle was improving slowly. On the advice of Dr Gowans and the insistence of his great-granddaughters he had been resting it, but there was a limit to his patience. He allowed the girls to settle him in a chair on the terrace while they cleared up in the kitchen and made the beds. He had every intention of getting about the garden as soon as they were out of sight on the dog-walk.

The drone of a vacuum cleaner soothed him halfway back to sleep. Wonder of wonders, the girls were tackling the housework! They had adjusted to his wishes almost without being told. He must have done something very good to be gifted with such paragons although just for the moment he couldn't think of anything of such magnitude. Keith Calder found him nodding as he dreamily contemplated his luck. Jane brought out another chair.

There was an unfamiliar wariness about Keith. He stood and looked around at the trees that formed the background to Luke's simple garden before he sat down.

Luke's drowsiness made a sudden departure. Keith's attitude had been that of a cowboy when Indians were around. 'Is something up?' he asked.

'It is indeed. Ike Johnson's temper, that's what's up.'

'Who?'

'Ike Johnson. Manager and part-owner of the Glenamis Hotel.'

'Oh him!' Luke said. 'I didn't know his name. What's got up his nose?'

Keith looked at him sharply. 'You'd better take this seriously. He's in the middle of a very smelly divorce just now. His wife owns half the hotel and she's going after him for his half on the grounds of irretrievable breakdown and mental cruelty, all the usual intangibles. Ike was sure that he was shit-proof because he was insisting on DNA proof that their baby was his and she was flatly refusing to provide a sample. While the lawyers did their stuff he felt safe to start a very canny affair with Emily Highsmith.'

Luke began to feel an uneasiness in his guts. 'How do you know all this?' he asked.

'Perhaps you forget that Ian Fellowes is my son-in-law. What I presume you don't know is that Dorothy Johnson was at school with Molly. They remain bosom buddies.'

'I see.' Luke took a few seconds to consider the implications. 'Yes, this is for taking seriously. He and Emily were lovers, if love really came into it. And then somebody as yet unspecified injured Emily so seriously that she seems unlikely to make it. She had played fair with him and kept their romance secret. But somebody had seen her with him and recognized him again at the hotel. There were just enough whispers going around so that when your blasted son-in-law persuaded me to help him, I tracked down that witness and identified the secret lover as Ike Johnson. Presumably your son-in-law has visited him and asked some pointed questions. Well, we both know how gossip flies around.'

'Don't we just?' Keith said with feeling. He had been subjected to almost as much as his fair share.

'Your son-in-law may have accidentally – or on purpose – dropped my name. Or somebody phoned somebody else and the connection, Mrs Benton's sister to Mrs B to me to DI Fellowes, became clear. If you take me out of the equation the tender secret could have remained just that. So he blames me for his wife finding out about his love-life?'

'And it looks like costing him a hell of a lot of money,' Keith said. 'Somebody seems to have whispered it to her lawyers. Remember, there's half-shares in a prosperous hotel in dispute.'

'He will not be pleased.'

'He isn't. I'm told that he's beating his chest. He always did have a temper. He's had to bottle it up for the last few years, because when the license comes up for renewal the police might express reservations if the manager, part-owner and licensee of a medium-sized but upmarket hotel had a habit of losing his rag.'

To Luke, this sounded worse and worse. If Ike Johnson was in danger of losing his grip on the hotel he might well also be losing his grip on his temper. 'He's a tough customer, is he?'

'And rough with it. So as soon as I got the word I hastened to warn you. If you have any weapons in the house, or anything that you could use as a weapon, keep it handy.'

'Shouldn't I ask for police protection?'

'You could ask,' Keith said, 'but I don't see them being much help. What could you tell them? He hasn't done anything yet. He hasn't even directly threatened you. All you have is my statement that Molly says Dorothy says that he's breathing fire and slaughter. I was trying to get hold of Ian earlier but I thought that it was more important to warn you and I don't have your mobile number. Now that I've warned you, I'll buzz off and look for Ian. If I tell him what's happening he may be able to get something moving – if not police protection then at least somebody could have a serious word with Ike and warn him of the consequences of attacking a man roughly twice his age. I'll make that point when I speak to Ian.'

Luke felt a sudden rush of affection for the man who could turn out to be such a good and energetic friend. 'Tell your son-in-law that he owes me that much help.' An idea had been trying to attract Luke's attention, distantly, as if he had been speaking to somebody at the front door while another visitor was knocking at the back. Now it entered uninvited. 'Could Ike Johnson be getting so uptight because he killed Emily? Look at it this way. He had a top-secret love affair. They were due to meet on the Friday night for purposes of adultery. They meet and there's a quarrel. "If you're going to treat me like this," Emily says, "I'm going to tell your wife what's been going on." More words are exchanged and she drives off, homeward. She's very upset and she's decided to leave contacting Mrs Johnson until she's calmer and more in control of herself. She thinks that she'd carry more conviction that way. But she's very upset and she pulls off the road until she feels calm enough to drive.

'That allows Ike to get to Birchgrove first and...' His voice died away.

'Yes,' Keith said. 'Now you see the snag. That was a possible theory all along, but I've never seen him in anything but an Audi. He couldn't lurk in the garage court in that without being noticed and he certainly didn't use it to damage Mrs Highsmith.'

Luke was not going to abandon without a fight any theory that solved the mystery of Emily's death and at the same stroke would almost certainly remove the angry Ike Johnson from the scene. 'I've never been inside the Glenamis Hotel but I've seen their advertising. Only to sneer at the rotten photography, but I've seen it. Do I remember that they can offer their guests shooting and fishing? If so, there must be a ghillie or a keeper, or both, complete with Land Rover. If their trysting place was near the hotel, he could easily have had time to swap vehicles and still get to Birchgrove before Emily did.'

Keith snapped his fingers. 'You have a point there,' he said. 'I'm ashamed to admit that I'd forgotten that they took over the sporting rights to the Glenfirnie Estate last year, when Jock Linklater died. They've been buying their cartridges elsewhere and so I've been putting them out of my mind. I think Ike acts as his own keeper and ghillie, bringing in occasional help from outside, but that does suggest that there's a Land Rover or a Land Rover substitute handy. I'd better go and find Ian. I suggest that you and your great-granddaughters go for a long drive in that new vehicle of yours and phone me before coming back again.'

Luke struggled to his feet. 'That's exactly my intention.' But when he listened he realized that the noise of the vacuum cleaner had stopped. There was no sound of voices, no radio playing, no thumping of heavy young feet. Even the birdsong seemed to have cut off. 'Where have they got to?'

'I think they went off with your dog a few minutes ago. They waved to you from the edge of the trees.'

'They've probably gone to do your dogging-in for you,' Luke said. 'I'd follow them up in the car but the trouble is that there are three different ways they could go. I'll have to wait here for them.'

Keith nodded. 'That's probably best. I'll go and hunt up my son-in-law. First, we exchange mobile numbers.'

'Quite right. Thanks. You're a good pal.'

Keith grinned. 'I'm only good because I'm getting old. It doesn't seem to have affected you, though.'

Luke was unsure whether to believe that the threat was real. He had occasionally been subjected to verbal abuse but physical threats had been as remote as the chance of being struck by a falling asteroid. Even so, elementary caution suggested that he should make himself and the girls scarce until tempers had had time to cool. He was too old for getting into punchups, and had been so for some years.

Until the girls made a return, he could do little but wait. He thought of locking himself into the house or the car, but such a move might only invite damage and cause an angry man to pick up something hard and heavy. His ankle was behaving well. In the end he decided to get on with whatever task he had intended to tackle next. This, conveniently, had entailed carrying at least one hammer with him. He made sure that his mobile phone was switched on in his pocket and fetched a few tools. As an afterthought, he keyed in the number of Keith's cellphone so that he would only have to press the green key to dial out.

Behind his usual parking place at the gable of the house, at just the right distance from the back door, there was a timber enclosure. This enclosed a small toolshed, a composting area and his barrows and other of the large items of garden equipment. The composting area, which also housed his refuse bins, was netted over to deter the deer that sometimes came to forage when times were hard. The enclosing fence was well built and looked like lasting for ever, except that one top rail had been in a different timber and had begun to rot. The local timber merchant knew Luke – he had supplied him with a special piece of timber several years earlier from which Luke had fashioned new handles for his two hammers. Luke was engaged to take the photographs of the timber merchant's golden wedding and had seized the chance to mention his need of a replacement rail. It chanced that the remainder of that earlier timber, which happened to be just about the right size, was still kicking around in the yard and Luke was presented with it.

The species of timber was uncertain, which is why it had never been used, but Luke rather thought that it was some sort of elm. After its years of seasoning it was certainly very hard, almost as hard as iron. Too hard, really, for the handle of a hammer; if he struck anything hard and heavy with his larger hammer, the stinging shock came back up the handle as if he had been caned across the palm.

He took his cordless drill out with him and drilled pilot holes for the first of his ring-barbed nails. He soon had the top rail fastened to the first three posts. He would be able to go faster now.

He was so absorbed that he never heard the car slide up and stop beyond the house. He only knew that he had company when a black shadow loomed in the corner of his eye. He looked round quickly. A large man with a bushy moustache had arrived and was approaching. He had no hat and could be seen to be totally bald. Even so, there was no doubt that he was physically fit and also angry. He stopped on the other side of fence. This, almost waist high, formed a demarcation rather than a real barrier.

'You're Luke Grant.' It was a statement rather than a question so Luke felt no need to reply. The man's eyes were popping. His face was infused with the dark blood of temper so that each of a dozen veins stood out purple. This, combined with a blue chin, made it a colourful face and therefore somehow more intimidating. 'You've been spreading muck about me.'

'I haven't spread anything,' Luke said. He noticed that his mouth had dried. His voice was husky. 'I've done nothing but look for the truth and I've spoken to nobody but Detective Inspector Fellowes.'

'Whose mother-in-law is pals with my wife! You wanted a truth, you've found one. The truth is that I'm going to break you in half.' The man's voice was rising in anger until he was shouting. His hands had closed into fists so that his knuckles had whitened. 'Well? Nothing to say for yourself? Don't think that being most of a hundred years old will save you. When you're too old to fight you'd be well advised to keep your head down.'

Luke had lost his voice but he found it again. 'Think what you're doing to yourself.'

'What the fuck do you mean?'

'You'll never get your license renewed. All you'll do is prove your own guilt. You'll be convincing everybody that you killed Emily.'

'My chances of keeping the hotel are as good as gone,' the man roared. 'I would never have hurt Emily,' and he swung a leg over the fence.

Luke acted without reasoned thought although the fact that he had, a few seconds earlier, rashly struck the last blow to a nail while his hand rested beside it may have affected his intuitive action. His hand was still smarting from the backlash. Let us be charitable and believe that Luke wanted no more than to demonstrate that he was in a position to defend himself.

While Johnson was sitting astride the fence, Luke swung the larger of his hammers. The man was too concerned with avoiding what he thought was a blow to his head to think of raising his most tender parts off the timber. Luke's own hand suffered a sting like that of a dozen hornets. For a second, Johnson failed to react, being unsure where the pain was coming from but knowing exactly where it was going. He uttered a single screech of agony but he was momentarily uncertain quite what was wrong and what would be best to do about it. This gave Luke time to take a second whack at the top rail and to his shame he did so.

In less than an instant the man lost his high colour. He shot his breath out so precipitately that snot hit his chin. His eyes were tight shut but a rush of tears began to escape. He took his weight off the top rail so that Luke's third whack at the rail was ineffective. Johnson's first attempts to get off the fence were handicapped by an inability to swing up either leg. After several attempts he managed to dismount by rolling backwards and then sideways to land with a thump at Luke's feet, still clutching the damaged area.

'You didn't have to do that,' he croaked.

'Yes I did,' Luke said simply.

'You hit me.'

'I didn't. And you were threatening me. I'd have been quite justified...'

It was an exchange that could have gone on indefinitely. Johnson seemed to prefer action. Some of the colour had returned to his face and he had managed to blink back the tears. He tried to struggle to his feet. Luke was confronted with choices between standing his ground, taking to his heels or whacking the other man with one of his hammers. He chose flight. Carrying both hammers rather than leave either as a weapon for his enemy, he swung one leg and then the other over the fence and made off across the grass with more pace than he would have believed himself capable of in his damaged state. As he went he groped for his mobile phone and jabbed at the green key.

Johnson was hot in pursuit but he was making little impression on Luke's lead because he was still quite sure that bringing his knees together would result in friction. If he had thought at all it would have been that his testes would strike like a match.

Luke had the impression that his own minutes were numbered. Either Johnson was beginning to recover from the shock to his genitalia or his fury was overcoming the pain, while Luke's own ankle was worsening and he could feel the first signs of angina. In addition, his few days of enforced idleness were counting heavily against his fitness. A half-heard sound suggested that there was a voice on his cellphone so he dragged it out, gasped 'He's here,' in its general direction and then pocketed it again.

They were on their second or third lap of the lawn – Luke had lost count – and he imagined that he could feel Johnson's hot breath on his neck. He was about to turn and swing either or both of his hammers when he was saved by the return of the dogging-in party.

The two girls, emerging round the corner of the house, were momentarily stunned by the spectacle of a limping man being pursued by another who was handicapped by trying to run bandy-legged. Pepper, however, took in the situation at a glance. Her beloved owner, who had fed her, loved her, worked her and protected her from attacks by rougher dogs and cattle, needed her help. She raced across the lawn. Her grab at Johnson's ankle missed but in running between his legs she tripped him. Johnson fell hard, rolled over and tried to sit up. The observers were in no doubt that he had set back the recovery of his damaged parts.

Luke beckoned Jane to him. He took two deep breaths. 'My pills and stick,' he croaked. He pushed the lighter of his two hammers at Violet and pointed at Johnson.

'You want me to dot him one?' Violet asked.

Luke took another three deep breaths and said, 'Only if he tries to get up.'

'On the head?'

Luke nodded.

'Hard?'

Luke had recovered some more of his breath. 'Not first time,' he said. 'Then, if he still tries to get up, hard as you like.'

'I can do that,' Violet said grimly.

Luke had found a convenient tree to lean against and breathe. 'So you should,' he said. 'He killed your mother.'

Johnson gave a grunt of protest. He tried to scramble up. Violet began to swing the hammer and he subsided hastily. 'I didn't,' he protested. 'I didn't, I didn't. I told you, I loved her.'

On the point of saying 'Balls!' Luke realized that in the circumstances the expression was a little too apt. 'Rubbish!' he substituted.

'I did! When my divorce was final we were going to be married. Then I'd have been your daddy,' he added to Violet. 'You'd have liked having a daddy again.'

'No I wouldn't,' Violet retorted, making an involuntary movement with the hammer.

'Perhaps not,' Johnson said hastily. 'Anyway, I didn't lay a finger on your Mum.' He paused and screwed up his eyes for a moment, aware that the expression was not the happiest but reluctant to emphasise it by choosing another. 'We did have a date for that evening but in the end I couldn't get away.'

Jane returned with his pills. Luke took one under his tongue. The threatened pain went by without stopping. He leaned on his stick and took his weight on his good ankle. 'You couldn't get away,' he said. 'And she was furious. She threatened to tell your wife everything.'

'Not true,' Johnson said. 'I told her that I couldn't get away. She...' He glanced anxiously at Violet. 'She asked whether, if she took a room, I couldn't join her for a little while; but I was committed, I didn't know for how long. She was annoyed but she went away saying that I was to phone her.'

'She went away threatening to inform Mrs Johnson,' Luke said. 'You followed her up and actually passed her when she pulled off the road. You were waiting for her in the hotel's Land Rover when she got back to Birchgrove.'

Johnson had gone from attack to defence. 'The hotel doesn't have a Land Rover. It has a bloody great four-wheel-drive Mercedes pickup truck that would have stuck out like a bishop in a four-ale bar.'

Luke was spared the problem of finding an immediate answer by the arrival of a small police car that disgorged three officers. This was followed by DI Fellowes's own car and then by Keith in Molly Calder's Suzuki. At the first sign of the rescuing cavalry, Violet hid the hammer under a rhododendron bush.

Johnson struggled to his feet. 'He hit me,' he said plaintively.

Luke had had enough. 'I did not. Show them a bruise. He threatened me. He said he was going to break me in half. And he was going to try it. He was stepping over my fence to get at me so I whacked the fence.'

Ian Fellowes stepped into the middle of the ring that had formed around them. 'Now, calm down, both of you, and tell me what's going on.'

Naturally they both started to speak. The DI held up a hand as if to stop traffic. Surprisingly, it worked. 'One at a time,' he said. He pointed at Luke. 'You kick off.'

Luke gathered his thoughts and went back to what he thought of as Square One. 'I brought you the identity of Mrs Highsmith's lover. You must have interviewed him. Then or at some other time his wife heard about it. She's part-owner of the hotel and she means to have his half off him. I presume you let my identity slip out. He came up here in a fizzing temper, either because his secret's reached his wife or because he killed Emily. He was going to break me in half. How do you *like* that?'

'Very little,' said the DI coldly. 'I interviewed Mr Johnson in absolute privacy. I did not release the identity of my informant, but it must have been well enough known. He couldn't have broken you in half though he might have tried, and the threat may be remembered if he's the next applicant for a renewed license. And he did not kill your granddaughter-in-law because there was a fight in the bar of the hotel that night between two groups of football fans and he was busy sorting it out and making statements until after midnight, after which there was some damage to clear up. None of which came to my attention until I visited him. All right.' He rounded on the uniformed officers. 'You three go away and get on with whatever you were doing when I called on you. There will be a report but no charges.'

'Thank you,' was all that Luke could find to say.

'Not at all. Now, can I trust you two idiots not to reopen hostilities as soon as my back's turned?'

'I'll see that they behave,' said his father-in-law.

The DI looked around the three men. Then he turned and walked back towards his car. Johnson approached Luke. Luke, unfamiliar with human reactions to violence but aware how a dog defuses an attack, prepared to fall on his back but Johnson put out his hand. 'Sorry,' he said.

Luke studied his face and decided that he

was sincere. They shook.

When Luke, the two girls and Keith had the place to themselves they turned to the house and took seats on the terrace. At Luke's direction, Jane fetched beers and some lemonade for shandy. Violet brought Luke a footstool and then collapsed into a chair. 'I was never so scared, GG,' she said. Her voice was shaking and she was close to tears.

'Of course you were, darling. A violent and angry man can scare almost anybody.'

'That wasn't it. I was scared that I was going to hit him. I'd seen him chasing you and I was so angry that I could have knocked his head off.'

'A very proper emotion when your great-grandfather is being threatened,' said Keith.

'How true,' said Luke. 'Violet, any time that you see a younger man chasing me, feel free to knock his head as far as you can and then spit down the holes in his neck.'

'GG!' said Jane. 'That's disgusting.'

Fourteen

Violet appeared in the French window. 'GG, Mrs Chambers is here. She would like a word with you.' Luke and Helena disengaged hands. 'Who's Mrs Chambers?' he asked Helena.

'An old lady. Lives alone in Birchgrove, on the downhill side of the garage court. Her husband died about a year ago. Shall I leave you to it? I could go and doll myself up.'

'Whatever you like. No need to hurry away before we know what she wants to say. Invite her in, please,' Luke asked Violet, 'and bring another chair.'

Mrs Chambers turned out to be a lady who Luke judged to be almost his own age, but she had not worn quite so well. Her hair was silver, she was slightly stooped and her facial skin had seen rather too much sunshine. She leaned on a stick and lowered herself into the proffered chair with the stiffness of arthritis. 'I apologise for bursting in on you like this,' she said, 'but I'm moving away very shortly. I shall miss Birchgrove, but there comes a time for sheltered housing and both my daughters are living near Elgin now.'

There was something familiar about her voice. When he looked closely he began to recognize her underlying bone structure. 'Haven't we met before?' he asked.

'I wouldn't expect you to remember,' she said. 'It was a long, long time ago.'

Luke pushed his memory further back. When he reached the year after Hannah's death, it clicked.

Luke had met a client in the Strathyre Hotel in Penicuik. It happened that a corporate entertainment was taking place in the same hotel at the same time. His business discussion was interrupted by music, laughter and applause. When he had concluded his business he walked out to the car park, which was shining with rain. There he found a couple of about his own age in evening dress, arguing beside a new-looking Rover. The man was swaying, obviously very close to the point of falling down.

The woman, an attractive lady, younger than her companion but about Luke's age, caught his eye. She was wearing a long dress of black velvet and a good fur coat. 'Would you help me, please? I'll have to get this idiot back inside and phone for a taxi. Or – haven't I seen you around in Newton Lauder?'

'I live there,' Luke admitted.

'I can drive,' the man said. 'Still capable. Whoops!' He swayed wildly and saved himself by a clutch at his companion.

'In a pig's ear,' said the lady, who turned out to be his wife. 'You drive in your present state and you'll be banned until you're five hundred years old.' She returned her attention to Luke. 'Could you give my husband and me a lift, do you think? I don't give much for our chances of finding a taxi at this time of a wet weekday evening.'

'I would be delighted,' Luke said, 'but I only have a sports car. A two-seater,' he added in explanation.

She looked at him measuringly. 'We could manage,' she said. 'We're none of us big across the bum. Or you could take him and I'll drive our car. I've only had a couple of sherries and a lot of lemonade.'

'I'm an obliging sort of chap,' Luke said, 'but I draw the line at being alone in my car with a total stranger who's obviously pissed out of his mind.'

'Who are you calling pissed?' the man demanded. This time he was saved by an obliging lamp standard.

'I see what you mean,' his wife said. 'We'll have to try to fit into your car.'

'It's been done before,' said Luke. 'Not including a lady in evening dress, but we'll try.' His business had concluded satisfactorily, so he was in an obliging mood.

A few seconds of study assured Luke that they would never manage the attempt with the top up. There was a *porte-cochre* over the hotel door. He moved his car under it and left the car in gear so that he could leave the handbrake off and out of the way. He put the fabric top down. Between them they moved the man into the passenger's seat. His wife tried to fit herself into the space behind the seats but even if there had been room there would clearly not be enough headroom to put the top up.

'We'll have to run with the top open,' Luke said.

'Not in a million years,' said the lady. 'You

wouldn't believe what I spent on this dress, let alone my hair. All to impress his boss. Well, he'll be impressed all right now. Impressed right out of his bloody mind, I should think. I'll come in the middle.' She climbed over the seats and settled herself, one buttock on each seat. Luke put the top up again. Little more than a hand's span of the driver's seat was left for him to occupy, but by persuasion followed by brute force he made his two passengers squeeze up until he could follow them inside and just force his door shut.

It was when he was ready to drive off that the remaining difficulty became apparent. The gear lever was somewhere under the lady's thighs. But she remained adamant. They were in, they were going home and no way was she travelling with the top down. She pulled up her skirt until the gear lever emerged coyly from under the black velvet. Luke drove off. The gear lever in neutral was between her stocking-tops, or rather higher in second and fourth gears. He soon stopped bothering to remove his hand between gear-changes. A rather pleasing vibration was transmitted from the gearbox. She whiled away the journey by cursing her spouse in an inspired variety of epithets, which he either ignored or failed to hear.

All too soon they arrived in Newton Lauder. Luke rather thought that the lady directed him by an unnecessarily circuitous route. They stopped at last outside an expensive bungalow in a quiet street backing on to farmland. Between them they wrestled the now comatose husband out of the car and supported him into the house. They settled him in a fireside chair, which she had turned to face the curtained window.

Luke was in no doubt that they, the lady and himself, were both thoroughly aroused by the manner of their travelling. When she whispered into his ear, he could detect the quickness of her breathing. 'This way, if he wakes up, we can be quite respectable in a couple of seconds.' She turned and rested her elbows on the chairback, with her jaw laid affectionately against her sleeping husband's bald spot.

Luke snapped back into the present. 'I remember you perfectly,' he said. 'Are you looking for another favour?'

She smiled. 'It may be time for me to

return the favour. I heard about the injury to Emily Highsmith and that you've been looking into it. I have some information. It may or may not be helpful, but I think I should tell somebody.'

'You should give it to the police,' Luke said.

'The removers are coming the day after tomorrow, first thing in the morning. I've just got back from a visit to my younger sister, who's had a heart attack but not as bad a one as she was making out. I have tomorrow, plus anything that's left of today, to sort through my late husband's things, which I've never had the heart to go through properly. I have to decide what comes with me, what gets thrown away and what might be worth selling. And I have to do the same for my own things. And the furniture. Well, to put it in a nutshell, I have a great deal to do and no time whatever to waste in talking to a lot of hidebound policemen. I've been there before and I know how they can waste time, passing you from person to person and taking statement after statement. I'll talk to you, now, or they can send somebody to Elgin.'

'Perhaps I should go,' Helena said.

'Not on my account,' said Mrs Chambers.

'I'd prefer you to stay,' said Luke. 'Your memory is often better than mine.' He turned to the visitor. 'So tell us what you saw.'

'I didn't see a thing. But I heard a lot. My arthritis often prevents me sleeping lying flat. Sometimes I'm better sitting up. I have a very comfortable chair beside my bedroom window. Some nights I fall asleep again immediately in the chair and don't remember a thing about my waking moments. But other nights, when it's very painful, I wake up suddenly and completely and it's as if some sort of a VCR was switched on in my brain and I can remember every sound, with accompanying vision if there's any light at all. I think it's my mind's way of turning away from the ... the discomfort. Friday night was like that. It was one of my worst nights ever and I can recall every detail. It was dark but it was hot and I had my window open.

'From about ten p.m. there was mostly silence except for footsteps. Those were mostly dog-walkers and one man who goes visiting while his wife's at the bingo and his ladyfriend's husband is playing bridge. Then it was so quiet that I heard a clock striking, down in the town, and I looked at my watch and it was about eleven. A little while later a car – it sounded like one of the ubiquitous Land Rovers – drove into Birchgrove and I heard it stop outside somebody's house.'

'Have you any idea which house?'

'None at all. Sound arriving through a window doesn't give you much sense of direction. Just after that, footsteps went past my house. I took it for another dog-walker. I think they turned down the rough road that joins the road up from the town. A few minutes later another Land Rover, or it might have been the same one, went down the same way; I heard the engine and saw the lights. There was some kind of an argument – I heard the sound of a horn, the vehicle stopped suddenly and there were raised voices, but they definitely weren't in the garage court where they found Mrs Highsmith and I couldn't make out a word that they said. Then the vehicle went on down to the bottom and a minute or two later I heard footsteps coming back.'

'The same footsteps?' Luke asked.

'I think so. They were light and short like a woman's. And a voice was talking as if to a dog. They faded away or just plain stopped.

'After another few minutes a car, a Land Rover again I think, started up somewhere in Birchgrove and drove round and into the garage court. I heard somebody pull up the metal door and then drive the vehicle inside. I expected to hear them slam the car door and come out and close the garage door again, but there was quite a long silence.

'The next thing was what sounded like a Land Rover came labouring up the steep track. Before it reached the garage court I heard an up-and-over door being opened by an electric motor. I think Mrs Highsmith has the only garage with a remote-operated electric door, am I right?'

'I think so,' said Luke. 'Go on.'

'The vehicle turned into the garage court and I heard it being put away in its lock-up. There was a pause before a car door slammed and the footsteps came out, walking more heavily as if carrying something. The electric motor went to work again, closing the big door. I could hear the footsteps and I think they were going towards the closed end of the garage court.

'Then I heard another Land Rover, the first one I think, start up. It drove out of its lock-up, turning, and then stopped and went into reverse. I could tell that it was reverse because it was a much lower gear and noisier. The noise went up and up as if the vehicle was hurrying, then suddenly I heard the squeal of brakes and the sound of a bump. I think the driver got out because after a few seconds of nothing much the car's door slammed, the driver revved the engine – isn't that what you say? – and let the clutch out with a bang so that the tyres yelped, and I heard it drive off.

'A little later I heard a Land Rover coming back up the hill. It could have been the same one or another, I've no way of knowing. It went into one of the lock-ups and the door was pulled down. Then I heard a woman's voice with pauses as if she was on the phone.'

'That would have been me,' Helena put in.

'Ah well,' said Mrs Chambers, 'from there on, you know the story better than I do. I felt that I had to tell somebody and that's what I've done. Now I'm going to get on with my life. If the police want to come and ask for more details, they'll find me at home tomorrow or in Elgin after that.'

'I didn't hear a car,' Luke said. 'How will you get home?'

'I have one of those little electric buggies. It's been a godsend.'

They saw her on her way. She gave Luke a faint, secret smile that said it all. They retreated back to the terrace. Helena lent him an arm. Luke waited until they were both seated. He looked to ensure that neither of the girls was within earshot.

'Why did you do it?' he asked.

Fifteen

He was still holding her hand. He felt her jump. 'Do what?' she asked.

He spoke gently. 'You know perfectly well. A lot of small facts had been coming together, suggesting one particular explanation. What Mrs Chambers said put the lid on it. She heard your Land Rover coming up the hill. That isn't the way you'd arrive, coming from my house, unless you'd been down to Ledbetter's to wash the back of your car.' Luke paused as another implication struck him a hammer-blow. 'Please tell me that you didn't do it for my sake. I couldn't bear that.'

'I didn't do it for your sake,' she said. 'I didn't do it at all. I would have done it if you'd wanted it, but I didn't think you did. Why would you think I did?'

'I haven't thought it all out yet, but Shaun comes into it. You told us that he died on

Thursday but...' He broke off suddenly as Violet arrived in the French windows bearing a tray with three cups.

'Oh, she's gone,' Violet said. 'Never mind, one of you can have two.' She smiled and then shook her head. 'You know, I don't think that could be right, about Shaun. Aunt Helena – she asked us to call her that – has one of those rotary things for dispensing medicines. A pill mill, it's called. It has separate compartments for each day and they're divided into morning, afternoon and evening. That's so that you don't forget and you always know which you've taken. She had it for Shaun, to remind her that he had pills for his arthritis and steroids to stop him scratching and he also got Windeze, because he did fart like nobody's business. And I noticed while we were round there that the pill mill was still in the kitchen and Thursday's and Friday's medicines had all gone. Saturday's and Sunday's were still there.'

Carrying the empty tray, she turned back.

'Go and get Jane and tidy your rooms,' Luke said.

'GG, how do you know that they're not tidy now?'

'One, it would be a miracle. Two, we have

a bargain – nothing but the truth, remember? If they were tidy, you'd have said so instead of asking a question. Now go and do it. And close the doors,' Luke called after her as vanished back through the French windows. He heard them close. There were no other windows to that side.

Helena heaved a sigh that finished almost with a shudder. She seemed to be studying her feet. She released Luke's hand. Then she turned, closed her eyes and laid her forehead against his shoulder. 'It's a relief,' she said at last. 'You don't know what a hell it's been, acting every minute and waiting for the axe to fall. I'm a good actress but it's a strain. I'd better tell you and then you can get it over with. Let me think.'

While she thought, Luke could feel the tension throughout her whole being. 'When I left you on the Friday evening,' she said at last, 'it was nearer eleven fifteen than eleven forty-five, but when I thought about it later I was sure that you wouldn't have any idea of the time. You were tired and dopey with sleepiness from sex and wine, and the clock in your sitting room had stopped. I drove straight home and went in by the good road, you were quite right about that. I left the

Land Rover outside my front door and went for Shaun. He'd been asleep but he soon woke up at the prospect of a walk.

'He always enjoyed the way down towards the town though I wasn't so keen because it meant a stiff climb back. We headed down that way. I kept him on the lead. There was a moon above a layer of thin cloud. We were near the junction at the bottom and I was going to cross the B-road and take to a path through the rough ground beyond where I could let him off the lead. But there was a sudden blaze of light and the sound of a vehicle coming fast down the bumpy road from Birchgrove, the way we'd just come. It was bouncing so that the headlights went up and down. I called to Shaun to come out of the road, but you know how deaf he could be, especially if he wanted to. Anyway, he had just started to do his business.

'I hauled on his lead and – wouldn't you know? – his collar came off over his head. The lights were so near and bright that he was throwing a long, black shadow, but I ran to grab him.'

Luke grasped her hand again and she clung to it. 'You could have been killed,' he said.

'Well, I wasn't. But the same thought struck me. I realized in a twinkling that it wouldn't do Shaun any good if we were both killed. I tried to pick him up but he wriggled and I dropped him and then it was too late. I made a jump out of the way. The vehicle went by with its horn sounding, missing me by about an inch. But it didn't miss Shaun. There was hardly a bump, Shaun was small for a spaniel. The vehicle was a Land Rover. It slithered to a stop and your granddaughter-in-law put her head out and asked me if I was all right. She was quite abrupt about it, not apologetic at all.

'Shaun was trying to crawl to me – looking for reassurance, that was the irony of it. I don't know how I know that, but I do. I think it's part of the telepathic link that a dog can develop with a really loving owner. I was wearing my old raincoat. I took it off and picked Shaun up in it. He was whimpering but he tried to lick my face. I was shaking all over but I think my voice was quite steady. I said that I was all right but that my dog was badly injured. I said that we might be able to save him if she drove me straight to Marigold's husband, which wouldn't take minutes. She said she could not spare the time but she'd be back before too long and then she drove off into the town. Can you believe that?'

From what he recalled of Emily's attitude to life, he could well believe that not even an injured dog would turn her aside once her mind was made up, but he had more sense than to say so.

'I was totally panicked. This was the dog that had been everywhere, done everything with me for years. He had slept on my bed and eaten under my table. I cradled him in my arms and spoke to him as comfortingly as I could and I tried to hurry back up the hill, but the hill and the darkness were against me and I had to try not to shake poor Shaun. For a while I could hear him breathing and whimpering and feel the little movements that a living body makes. And then suddenly I couldn't. I turned towards where Mr Hicks lives but as I reached my own back gate I realized that there was nothing he could do, Shaun was dead and I was already exhausted.'

As if remembering her exhaustion, she slumped against him. 'I put Shaun down in the garden. As you know, my garden isn't overlooked; it's between the blank walls of

Mr Davis's summerhouse and Mary Kemp's studio. I noticed that Mr Schuster, who does the gardening for most of the houses in Birchgrove, had dug the hole for the lilac tree that I'd bought from the garden centre, just as I'd asked him to; but it's only a little wee tree and he'd dug a huge hole. He does tend to go over the top, Mr Schuster. That put the idea of a grave into my mind.

'The next thing was to put the Land Rover away. My insurers insist on it. So I got in and drove round to the garage court. I backed into my lock-up. And then I just sat there while the shock came over me. I was shaking. It hit me that I'd lost Shaun and now I was truly alone. Except for you, of course, but I never did deserve somebody like you. And a person who could have helped, who probably could have saved him, had refused. I began to boil. I think that I cried for a minute or two, which is something I don't often do.

'I was jerked out of my selfish despond by the sound of another Land Rover. It turned into the garage court and I heard an electric door opener at work. The only person with a Land Rover who has a remote controlled door opener is Emily Highsmith. I listened while she backed into her lock-up. She got something out of the back of the car and then I heard the door winding itself down again, just as Mrs Chambers said, and footsteps going towards the closed end of the garage court. I saw her walk past. As far as I could tell, she'd made no effort to see whether Shaun or I was still around and needing help.

'My blood came to the boil. My thoughts were swimming around and bumping together; I think the nearest I came to having a coherent thought was, "Let's see how she likes having a vehicle come at her out of the dark." I don't know why I first turned away from her except that that's the way I always have to turn. I saw her down at the far end of the court, quite brightly lit by my reversing light. So I slammed into reverse and went back. I had three mirrors to take aim by. I watched her get back against the wall holding a cardboard box in front of her as if that would stop me. Her face shone white.

'My senses returned to me. It happened in an instant, like a revelation on the road to Damascus. All in that moment I realized that Shaun was a darling but he was only a dog and he was old and it was quite a quick end and he'd died in my arms as he'd have wanted. And I'd already done what I intended and showed her what it was like to be rushed at by a Land Rover. I stamped on the brakes, but what I hadn't realized or I'd forgotten was that my brakes are much less fierce going backwards than going forwards. Mr Ledbetter tried to sort it out but he didn't make much difference. I hadn't quite come to a stop before there was a heavy bump from behind me and the Land Rover jerked to a halt. I pulled forward a few feet and got out. I stopped the engine, leaving the car in reverse. By my reversing light I could see much more than I told you and the inspector later. I could see that she was crushed. I thought that if she wasn't dead she soon would be. I was wrong there, which must have meant a lot of extra suffering. That's the one thing that I'm really sorry about.

'In an instant it came to me what I had to do. The whole plan was crystal clear in my mind. It was simple but it needed luck if I was to do it without being seen and identified. The late-night traffic of home-goers would start soon so I had to hurry. I closed my garage door, got back into the driver's seat and drove quickly down the hill to Ledbetter's. I was expecting at any moment to cross with another driver who would recognize me and my vehicle, but I never saw a soul. Ledbetter leaves his power hose available, mostly for the benefit of keepers and stalkers who've been out late and are headed for home with the vehicle plastered in mud. It took only seconds to blast the back clean. I dare say a full forensic examination could still have found traces, but it hasn't come to that yet and I went down again two days later and washed the car properly. I took the spare wheel off inside my lock-up and gave a good scrub behind it.

'As soon as I'd finished I hurried back up the hill and into the garage court. Nobody had arrived and found her. She was still there, of course. I put the car away, got out my mobile phone and called my sister. I let her call the ambulance while I put Shaun into the hole, still wrapped in my old raincoat, and planted the tree over him. It's a good place and I think he could be happy there. My sister had more than thirty miles to come and she's a slow driver, so I had time to wash and change my clothes. The raincoat had caught most of Shaun's blood but there was some on my skirt and I bagged it for disposal. I'm not saying where it is but it's gone now.

'Since then, I've been mad to think that I could get away with it and, like I said, I've been waiting for the axe to fall. It looked to me as if I was safe from the police, they were overstretched and disagreeing with each other.'

'Keep your voice down,' Luke said. 'We don't want the girls to hear any of this.' He had been following her every word. His mind was working full tilt, digesting the words and exploring the implications. 'It must have been you who tampered with my brakes. What was that about?' he asked sternly. 'I couldn't believe that you hated me but I can't think of anyone else with any kind of motivation, unless I was getting too close to the culprit without knowing it. Was that it? I was beating my brains out looking for whatever I'd missed.'

Her voice, when it came, sounded choked. 'I must have been mad. I couldn't ever hate you. I'm your slave, you must know that. But you were helping them and you knew a lot of locals. If you asked enough questions you would have started getting answers. But that wasn't even half of it. What terrified me was that Mrs Highsmith was still alive and she was asking for you. You were going in to Edinburgh to see her. If she was *compos mentis*, you would be the one person she might have confided in. But once, when you were arguing with another man, I heard you say that a competent driver should be able to cope with brake failure, using his engine and gearbox. I only had some vague idea of keeping you out of Edinburgh for the moment, while I tried to think of some longer-term solution. I was appalled when I realized the danger I'd put you into.'

He patted her shoulder. 'Now I understand,' he said. 'It's all quite logical once you know and understand.'

She heard the tremor in his voice and looked up suddenly. 'You're *laughing*?'

'Not really. The whole situation is far from funny. Just for a moment the cross-purposes looked a little amusing.'

They sat, leaning together. The shadows were stretching across the lawn. Each was deep in thought while trying to guess the thoughts of the other.

'So what happens now?' she asked at last.

'Do we go to the police together?'

He had made up his mind. 'You can go to the police if you want to,' he said. 'But I thought we had a date for tonight.'

'You mean—'

'I mean that I have no intention of being judge and jury. Let's think again from the start. It began when my half-baked grandson went and married quite the wrong woman. Thousands have done the same. Instinct is stronger than intellect. To do her justice she gave him two fine girls. But that does not make her a good person. Perhaps this is wishful thinking, but from what she said to me in the hospital and because she refused to say anything about who was to blame, I think that, like you, she had a revelation. If she'd lived she might have been a quite different person. But at that time, she was a bad one. Common decency and all the laws of behaviour should have obliged her to run you wherever you needed to take the dog that she'd injured, but a torrent of hormones was driving her towards her lover.

'You were provoked beyond endurance. I hope that I wouldn't have done the same, but I well might have done under such provocation. I believe your account of how it happened and I believe that you tried to stop.'

Helena sighed again. 'Thank God! You wouldn't believe what a relief that is. I couldn't have born it if you, of all people, condemned me. Whether a court will believe me, that's another matter. I would certainly plead guilty to leaving the scene of an accident. If hard-pressed, I suppose I'll have to admit to manslaughter. I only hope that it doesn't come to a conviction for culpable homicide.'

Luke gave her a little shake. 'You seem to be determined to have a trial. It may come to that, of course. But I think that Keith Calder will help me. If we both give DI Fellowes the opinion, based on local knowledge and after my talking to most of the denizens of Birchgrove, that it was an accident and a hit-and-run with nothing to identify the culprit, I think he'll be relieved to go along with his superiors in Edinburgh and agree. It will make his statistics look better.'

He felt her breathe out a long breath. 'I would never have dared to ask you to look after me. Something inside me kept saying that you probably would. But,' she continued in a very small voice, 'you can't change the fact that I did something awful. Has it turned you off me, knowing what I've done? Or do we still have a date for tonight?'

'I'm counting on it,' he said. 'I need a little loving too, now and again.' Daylight was almost gone but he could see the first tentative return of her smile. 'You were swept up in the kind of events that make people act out of character. But I know you too well to believe that the real you would act that way. I trust you and that's an end to the matter. Just remember this. You must never again utter a word about it. From your background as a legal secretary you must know how many people get convicted because they opened their silly mouths. You have nothing to say, to anybody, at any time.' He paused. She began to speak but he gripped her arm. 'No, not even to me. Nobody at all, ever. And now, you were going to go home and pretty yourself up. I need a shower and a shave. Come back soon and we'll show each other what love is all about.'

While he was in the bathroom he decided that his next application of the chilli pepper ointment was due and he remembered the doctor's advice to wash his hands immediately after using it and on no account to touch anywhere sensitive. The intimacy to come was at the forefront of his mind and he would have to have a care. He chuckled at a sudden thought. This, he decided as he rubbed the ointment in, would be a bad moment to become desperate to spend a penny.

The thought, of course, was father to the wish.